THE CAMERA

By Michael Lachance

The Long Short

McKinney Sweetlock

21 Windows

Three Fools for Spies

Treaty of Versailles, The Power of Love

The Camera by Michael Lachance

The Camera

Skipper Pete Books, PO Box 16, Glenwood, IA 51534

Print ISBN: 978-1370745814

Contents

Chapter 1: Memorial Museum of Verdun & Father Leauvin 6
Chapter 2: 1916, Verdun, France   14
Chapter 3: The Horse   25
Chapter 4: The Enemy   36
Chapter 5: Camaraderie   49
Chapter 6: The Attack on The Monster's Back   58
Chapter 7: Nighttime Cries   72
Chapter 8: Two Pictures, Two Men, One Woman   85
Chapter 9: Sophie Rousseau, Apt 9, Rue De Garibaldi-Paris 95
Chapter 10: Battle of Verdun   102
Chapter 11: The Camera   115
About the Author: 120

Chapter 1: Memorial Museum of Verdun & Father Leauvin

Present day France, the cannons aimed up, they sat right in front of the Memorial Museum of Verdun. Mama pulled at her son, barely thirteen. Her husband, a stout man with dark hair, looked at him. "Your great papa fought near here. We must know the past, so that we can live a good future."

"Yes, papa." He said. "How long are we staying?"

"Ah, there's the guide." Papa said.

"Welcome to the World War One Memorial of Verdun, France." His wrinkles were seventy, but his stature was fifty. "Je m'appelle Claude Verdot." His blue eyes passed over the faces, "in English, I'm Claude and your guide for this tour."

A couple of people sighed, a few laughed politely.

"So, you are here to learn about World War One and to have a memory of your visit." He headed into the gallery. The gallery was very big; half the size of a soccer field and in the center, there was a trench with barbed wire, a cart and mule, and some other WWI equipment. "This structure was built over this trench; the trench is authentic."

The boy looked over the second-floor rail. His eyes shot from one thing to another: the machine gun, the soldiers, the cart and mule and then the twisted remnants of barbed wire; his eyes widened. The only tree was just a blackened stick that reached out from the ground and begged for help.

"You look here and can almost hear the bombs." The man whistled so strong that it pierced the tourists' ears, but then the whistle slowly faded, "BOOM!" He shouted.

The boy jumped! And some of the tourists let out a sharp sigh from their anxiety.

"You hear it this time and it may be enough, but for the men there in the trenches, they suffered through hundreds of bombs dropped all around them and … on them." He whistled again and slowly the sound tapered off.

The boy covered his ears!

"BOOM!" The guide shouted, "Huge chunks of dirt and metal shards blasted from the ground." He threw his hands up. "And anyone that didn't get down …" He shook his head.

The boy pulled at his father's sleeve. "What's a shard?"

"Sharp pieces of metal," Father said and touched the boys shoulder.

The boy looked hard at the trenches and a gray mist spread over them; it headed toward the French soldiers. Then, men yelled! Bombs blew up the ground and threw dirt and shards of metal at the men! Machine guns roared! The boy closed his eyes and trembled. Then, the mist swallowed everything whole.

Paris, France – May 1916:

Father Leauvin stood at the steps to his church. He turned to look at the passersby or to give the impression that he looked at nobody. But, he looked at a woman. She dipped her head at him and smiled. His heart fluttered and his skin cooled. He gulped and then looked away, back to the church. A deep breath filled his lungs and he used it to push away the feelings that flooded him. The doors to the church were made of such solid wood that when he passed through them a small portion of the weight of the wood rested on his shoulders. Normally, he did not come through the main doors, but through the side street. Today was more profound and the side entrance didn't do justice to

7

his departure. Father was on his way to Verdun where the First World War shattered, shook, and ruined everything in its path.

He got his composure back and stood still for a moment at the vestibule. His cassock was clean and nicely pressed. A deep breath and then onwards through the church, his cassock swayed back and forth as he made his way past the pews. His hands were clasped together in prayer, but his mind slipped from war to the woman that nodded at him. He wiped at his mouth and then his forehead. The church felt hot, musty. He gasped for some air and then caught his breath.

The people in prayer heard nothing.

Father stopped, got his emotions pushed down deep into his gut and then stood straight. He walked to the stairway and descended quietly.

Bishop Manteau waited for him, but he had to check his things for the trip to the front. Something peculiar about Father Leauvin was that he owned a camera. He wasn't to mention it or be seen with it the bishop told him. What priest carries a camera and not his cross?

Father Leauvin clutched a small wooden cross in his hand as he made his way down the hall to his room. The door was open. A small tattered box sat on the floor next to a very neatly made bed. In the box, he'd put another cassock and one pair of street clothes. Next to the box was a dark brown hard case and he studied it closely, "Herbert & Huesgen, New Ideas Mfg. Co." His fingers ran along the name and felt each embossed letter, "merci … merci beaucoup mama and papa."

Then, he used his thumbs to force the snaps open. Slowly, the middle separated and the two sides gently fell apart. He was taken by what he saw and smiled so wide that his cheeks touched his ears, "easy." Inside was a camera wrapped in leather with a loose leather strap over the top to carry it with. There were a couple of knobs, a small crank to forward the film and a black lens with small black face numbers around the aperture. He smelled the leather and then checked the door. He thought to shut it, but to put down his camera hurt. He stood, went to the door and looked out. It was quiet. He turned back to his cell and got his hands firmly around the camera. He steadied himself and then looked through the viewfinder. It was too dark. He hurriedly turned the lantern up. Then, he steadied the camera and exhaled slowly, "click." He cycled the film until the next frame locked in place.

It was an odd thing for a priest to hold a camera close to his heart and not the cross; Father Leauvin meant no disrespect and it did not change how much he loved the Lord, but he hugged his camera. A moment passed and then there were words down the hallway; another priest or the bishop was near. He quickly boxed the camera up carefully and pushed the snaps closed.

The moment he stuck his head out the door, the bishop was in his face.

"Father Leauvin?" He looked around him to see if he was packed. "You're ready?" Bishop Manteau asked and the "r" rolled off his tongue with some held back spit so that he nearly gurgled the "r" when he said, "You're."

"Oui, Bishop Manteau." He nodded, got his cross in hand and then eased his smile.

"To smile so wide when you're on your way to the most dreadful place on earth is not holy." Bishop Manteau frowned.

"Oui, sorry your Excellency." Father bowed his head in reverence and followed the bishop into the hall. He very briefly looked back at his open door, smiled and then turned back to the bishop. They walked down the hallway and the heels of their shoes drummed a marching beat.

They were at Bishop Manteau's office. The bishop sat down behind a large desk; the wood was dark and the carvings looked gothic with gargoyles (so it appeared) carved out of the corners.

Father studied one gargoyle to be sure of it and then wondered how the bishop got the desk in here when he took in the whole of thing. "Larger than life," he said.

"What's that?" The bishop turned his head to hear.

Father cleared his throat, "sorry your Excellency … nothing."

"I worry that you're going to the front." He pulled at his collar. The heat from his large barrel shaped chest was intolerable. "You don't seem focused."

"Your Excellence," Father's backside felt hotter now, pricklier. "I …"

"You confound me with that camera and …" He widened his gaze as if to eat Father.
"A gift from my …"
"Parents, yes I know." He sat forward and tried to rest his elbows on his desk, but his chest and belly wouldn't allow it. "And that you have little to no compunction to interrupt me." He scoffed. "Are you a priest committed to Christ's work?"

Father's teeth gritted together and a bead of sweat was strung like Christmas lights across his forehead.

"Father Leauvin … that was a question." He shook his head.

"Sorry your Excellency, but you said not to interrupt." Father tried to smile, but half his face rose up and the other half frowned.

"You see, you border on impertinence and courtesy." He sat back and took his cross in hand tightly.

"I'm sorry." Father said, sighed and then wiped his forehead. "I'm a servant of God and I am committed to my life as a Christian."

"By following doctrine and your faith … in Christ." Bishop Manteau pushed back from his desk and opened the center drawer.

"Yes," Father said and felt his body tense up.

"Say it." He said, took a paper from his desk, got a quill and lifted the lid to the ink.

"Your Excellency?" Father's hands trembled.

"To err is human," he said and set the quill in a holder.

"To forgive, divine." Father smiled and was quite happy to say it.

"Non Father Manteau, non." The bishop brought his hands together. "Say … By following doctrine and your faith in Christ Jesus."

"Oh," Father cleared his throat and readied himself. "By following doctrine and your …"
"Non!" The bishop's rosy cheeks were redder, hellish looking. "Not your, my" He shook his head.

"Ah, of course." Father sweated. "By following doctrine and *my* faith in Christ Jesus."
"You see, that is all I asked of you." He got the quill and signed the paper. "But it is very much like trying to absolve the devil of sin with you." He sighed and sweat fell from his head; the droplets landed on the paper and bled some of the ink. The bishop got a vile of ponce and sprinkled the fine powder on his signature. Then, he gently blew at the powder. "You will take this letter with you and wherever you go."

"Yes, Your Excellency." Father's body eased.

Bishop Manteau forced a grin. "I know you mean well, but do be more thoughtful."

"I will." Father waited for the que to stand for dismissal.

"Your journey will take you into the devil's den." Bishop Manteau leaned back and tried to relax. "Verdun has the heaviest casualties and you must protect your soul and your body."

"Your Excellency?" Father raised his brows.

"The vile weapons of this modern era rip and tear men to pieces." He looked at a picture of Roman soldiers in a battle with the Gaul's. "I fear that their souls may be lost in the madness."

"I will help them." Father said.

"You must." He got the wax stick, heated the end and dabbed a spot on the letter. He pressed his ring onto it and then lifted his hand away. "There you are." He stood, got the letter and handed it to father. "Christ be with you."

Father stood quickly, "And with you." He took the letter and bowed his head.

Bishop Manteau nodded and Father backed up a step or two, turned and left.

In the next moment, he was in his cell and then down the hall and out the side door. A man with a wagonette waited for him.

"The bishop had a lot to say?" The man's hat was pulled down to just above his eyebrows. He was a sixty something who did not have the desire to wash more than once every couple of weeks.

"Oui, but he cares deeply." Father said and set his things in the wagonette.

The ride was solemn and Father thought on the bishop's words, "vile weapons," and "rip and tear." He prayed.

"For me too," the old man said. "On y vas!" He shouted at the horses and snapped the whip. The two horses jumped and broke into a fast trot. "Twill be at least two or three days for us."

"Very good," Father got his bible from his box.

"Very good for now, Father." The old man laughed to himself. "But when we get there, it will be the inferno of Dante."

Chapter 2: 1916 – Verdun, France

June 1916, nighttime, the battlefield of Verdun was an open wound filled with mines, gunfire and miles of tangled barbed wire. The French and Germans were firmly in their trenches. A French soldier, Philippe, held trench binoculars in hand and inched them ever so slightly above the sand bags that protected them from German bullets. He looked at a horse with its center blown out. The rider lay nearby with his hand pointed upward, dead. He lowered the binoculars and sat down.

Other men talked amongst themselves, some smoked, some cleaned their rifles and others thought about nothing. Better to think on nothing than to think about their lives before the war; a single shot would end any voyage home.

Philippe lit a cigarette and drew in a heavy breath. The orange glow brightened his dirty face. His cheeks hung unusually low for such a young man and his face had bits of dirt that were slightly embedded in his pores. No one thought to wipe their face off after German bombs landed nearby. His helmet sat cockeyed on his head and it would deflect a bullet or metal bits from a bomb. His rifle lay against the dirt wall; he could grab it and shoot in a couple of seconds if need be. He drew in another breath of thick smoke and then pressed his fingers hard against his sore eyes. A man stepped carefully around the men.

The man stopped and nodded after a quick chat with some men. Then, he moved towards Philippe. Philippe lowered his cigarette and studied the man. He spat and then shook off the cool air.

"Sergeant," the man said.

"Sir," Philippe set the cigarette on his rifle and then saluted.

The lieutenant saluted, turned and peered over the sand bags. Then, he quickly lowered his head.

"Sir," Philippe said firmly. "One shot."

"Oui, I know." The low light from a lantern showed the young lieutenant's face; he had the skin of a baby and strong cheeks. "Word from HQ is that a priest will join us."

Philippe tried not to shake his head with disappointment. "But, I've got my men to look after."

"Oui, I know." He stepped past Philippe and looked down the trench line. "Mais, Sgt. Lachance will take five or so of your men."

"Sir?"

He touched Philippe's shoulder. "You know the terrain, the enemy, and you have been very good to survive this long."

Philippe tried to smile. The lantern wasn't close enough to show his face, but the shadows showed that he wasn't happy about it. "No more charges then."

"I cannot promise that." The lieutenant smiled. "But, it is likely that the priest will not ever charge the enemy."

"Bien sur," Philippe said. "When does he arrive?"

"Perhaps … mid-morning or late afternoon." The lieutenant dipped his head.

"What's he like?" Philippe didn't dread the thought of looking after the priest, because he'd be freed from the whistle.

"Like a priest." The lieutenant said and then nodded.

Philippe stood at attention and saluted. He thought about the whistle as the lieutenant disappeared into the shadows.

When the whistle blew, the men leapt from the trench and charged the enemy. They faced bullets that punctured them, bombs that threw sharp metal at them and barbed wire that grabbed at them

Philippe swallowed hard. He'd faced the guns and the bombs many times.

The Germans wanted Verdun. It was a strategic location to capture at any cost. After the back and forth attacks, Verdun was a wasteland. But the darkness covered the scars of war like a blanket. Dark wavy berms were rolling hills, barbed wire were thorn bushes and demarcation posts were starving trees.

During the day time though, men's eyes were shocked by the destruction. The barbed wire ripped and cut them, demarcation posts were a hard warning that you could die sooner than later if you got close, and the berms were cover for the enemy.

Many hectares of land were pockmarked with deep holes blasted out by bombs. Trees were shredded so that just their wretched stump was left. Buildings were obliterated: splintered pieces of wood thrown all over, bricks thrust onto the land. The only remnants of homes were burned and riddled with bullet pockmarks. Philippe felt just a touch of happiness that he had a reprieve from the wasteland.

He took a small cross that hung from a necklace and kissed the cross. Then, he tucked it safely in his shirt and sighed. Back to now he thought and got his cigarette from the top of his rifle. He took a toke and then got his gas mask from a pouch on his hip. He put it on, blew out and then sucked in to get it to seal around his face.

A fellow soldier walked up and waved his hand at him. He spoke softly, "it's the newer one?"

Philippe nodded and removed the mask. "It is."

"You had a good seal?" The man asked.

"Indeed," he smiled and nodded. "You've checked yours?"

"Yes, but the men worry that mask was not tested here." He looked up and down the trench.

Philippe chuckled, "of course not." He put the mask away. "This is a rat's job."

"Four legs or two?" The soldier laughed.

Philippe looked at him with a more serious eye. "I believe they will work." He tapped the soldier's shoulder. "You've heard then Renault?"

"Of course, that's why I came." They sat down. "You are a lucky devil."

"With a priest," He chuckled.

"Well, be sure if it's my time …" Renault looked away.

"I will." Philippe nodded. The words that were on Renault's tongue were held back. If he's killed, be sure that the priest gives him last rites. Philippe finished his cigarette, looked at the small package with his last two cigarettes and shook his head, "non."

The night was surprisingly quiet. It was too quiet in fact. Most of the men slept for periods of no more than an hour or so. Anxiety woke them with thoughts that they were under attack.

The sun slowly edged up and shot an orange glow across the hilly ground. The soldiers did everything they could to get a touch of it on their face. Within an hour or so, orders would come and the bombing would start or, worse, they would line up along the trench wall to go on foot!

An attack on open field was the surest way to be shot or blasted to bits. Philippe drew in a heavy breath with his yawn and then rubbed his face hard. He went to a covered trench and threw some water on his face. The priest might arrive today.

Might arrive was the truth. To get through the patrols and, sometimes, the shifting lines was nearly impossible. Philippe hoped that he had papers on him. "Of course," he said and rinsed his mouth.

"Sergeant," a soldier said and dipped his hat at him.

"Vazant," Philippe nodded.

Vazant went to a basin and took his helmet off to wash some of the filth off.

Philippe got his helmet on, got a picture from his pocket and kissed it. "Sophie," he said and then put it back in his pocket. He walked down the trench. Most of the soldiers sat and busied themselves with a shave, music or talk, anything to take their mind from the task that lie outside the trench. He nodded at them or dipped his hat and made his way to HQ to see about this priest.

Philippe stopped at a pair of trench binoculars. He wiped his eyes and then looked through them. The dirt and the barbed wire only made noise when bombs or bodies hit them. Were the Germans going to attack? He looked at the line. "Attention!"

"BOOM!" A shell landed just a couple of meters away! Dirt and shards of metal blasted through the air!

Men rushed for cover! "BOOM!" German shells went up and then plummeted down to French trenches! Boom after boom rang in their ears until the ringing was all they heard! Philippe shouted and pulled at some men who didn't get to cover; they were too terrified to move! Then, French artillery whirred over their heads and the men shouted, "VIVE LA FRANCE!"

Philippe got back to the trench binoculars and looked again. There was so much smoke just ahead of them. "Fix bayonets!" He pulled the long metal knife from his side and fixed it to the end of his rifle. He'd done it before, but for most men the word alone was enough to turn their stomachs upside down. "Bayonets!" He got his whistle and blew one quick blow!

The men knew that they were not to go up as this was a preparation warning. They got their bayonets fixed and stood at the edge of the sand bags piled high along their trench.

The lieutenant waved at Philippe and then used the trench binoculars to have some idea of the Germans' advance.

The bombs stopped for a moment, but the French continued their artillery. The lieutenant dipped his head at Philippe. Philippe's stomach sank; he turned and went to the soldier at a machine gun. "Ready," he tapped the soldier's helmet.

"Oui!" The soldier got his hands around the handles tightly and eyed the ground ahead of him. He swung his barrel slowly to the right and hit the limiting stake. Then, he moved the barrel to the left and the barrel tapped the limiting stake. Then, he centered his machine gun. The soldier next to him had several belts of ammunition around his neck and held up the belt that fed into the machine gun.

"Calm," Philippe forced himself to smile at these teenagers.

"Oui, Sargent," the gunner said.

The lieutenant waved for Philippe to come to him.

Philippe jogged along and over the muck. He saluted and then leaned in.

"We've no word on an attack." He looked through the binoculars again. "It may have been a test to check defenses."

"Yes, I've seen nothing yet." Philippe kept his helmet below the sand bags. A sniper's round sometimes pierced a helmet as easily as a hot knife sliced through butter.

"I'm waiting on word from HQ." The lieutenant said and bit at his lip. He turned back to see if his runner was coming. "Damn the line of communication … Rossy!"

A man that barely stood to the underarm of the lieutenant ran up, "Sir!"

"A note to HQ, you are the fastest." He looked up and a French artillery round whirred by. "Any closer and they'll hit us."

"I hope not." Rossy said, "Sir."

"At last," the lieutenant said. The French artillery stopped. He walked to a covered trench and there was a small desk. "A quill … ah." He grabbed the quill, dabbed it in ink and scribbled a note. He folded it and handed it to Rossy. "Bon chance."

Rossy saluted, took the note, crawled up the pass and out from the trench. He was short and shockingly fast. In a second, he vanished into the ground behind them.

The lieutenant returned to where Philippe looked through the binoculars. "Nothing."

"Let's keep our guard, keep our watch, but wait for HQ." The lieutenant nodded and Philippe saluted. "Sargent."

"Yes?"

"No whistle, just man to man." The lieutenant nodded.

Philippe nodded and went to the man nearest him, "pass the word—keep your guard." And so it went that the message was passed man to man.

The lieutenant had some idea that the Germans knew their whistles and certain blows gave them information of an attack or to stand down. He did not want the Germans to hear anything.

Philippe wondered about the priest. Would he make it today with the bombardment? It was unfortunate that the bombing was more normal than the priest arrival. The commander may like the idea that the priest got to the front and lived for a few days.

It would be terrible to report that the priest was shot or a bomb hit nearby which cast his chest north and his head south. Philippe didn't mean to laugh, but the thought to send that message to HQ was to good to miss. HQ had no trouble to send them orders that were laughable. "A stalemate," must be broken in a message they got. To break the stalemate, Philippe and his men were sent into the open plain and charged the German line.

Philippe's stomach turned even now as he thought on the attack two weeks past. The lieutenant blew the whistle and they climbed from the trench, Philippe and forty or fifty men. Then, they charged ahead. Bullets and bombs were closer to them than the nearest man. The fall back whistle was blown only after half the men were hurt or killed.

He sniffed the end of his barrel and took in the strong scent of burned up gun powder. He pressed his fingers against his eyes when he thought on the terrified faces of men who lay on the ground. This man had been shot many times, that man's leg got ripped from his body by shrapnel, and another man's rifle lay at his side because his hand was just a red meaty chunk. Philippe spat.

It wasn't that the injuries made Philippe upset as much as the faces of men he tried to help. The shocked expression on their face when he shook his head at them; they would die in minutes. Other men, he grabbed wherever he could and pulled them back to the trench. Some of those men were shot in the leg or torn up by shrapnel.

Philippe spat again and then got a drink of water. The water did more than wash the dryness from his throat. It seemed to wash away some of the horrors too.

"Sargent!" The lieutenant shouted and motioned for him to come.

"Sir," he hurried to the command tent and walked in.

"So, Rossy has word." He set the note in the fire. Rossy saluted and left. "The Germans remain in their positions. It, they believe, was a ruse to draw us out onto the open ground."

"That would have been bad, Sir." Philippe said.

"Your priest is at HQ and they will send him this evening." The lieutenant walked to the back of the command tent, opened a sack and got a bible out. "Have you got one?"

"Yes, sir." Philippe nodded. "Have you got his name?"

"Ah, yes … it's Leauvin, Father Leauvin."

"Very good, the men will be in better spirits with a priest here." He said and sighed.

"Me too, Sargent." The lieutenant sat down and got a journal opened. "Give the all clear."

Philippe saluted, turned and left. His stomach growled and he thought about a horse not too far from them. "The meat," he mumbled. After he gave the all clear, he looked through field binoculars and saw the beast; its chest was blown open and the bare ribs showed. Under his breath, he counted the steps to the horse.

A soldier walked up, licked his thumb and then wiped the site post of his rifle. He held his finger up. "You can make it out." He tapped his jacket and dust rose up into his unshaven face.

"Yes, but to make it back with enough." Philippe said. He looked at the soldier. "Charles, it's possible to make the run from there." He pointed to a crater. "This will hide me until I'm behind it."

"Yes, but to work at it … they will see the horse move or your head and then." He made his hand into a gun and squeezed a trigger. "So, stay as low as is possible."

Philippe thought for a moment, "ah!" He hurried off.

"He's had the good idea." Charles said.

A moment passed and Philippe returned with some rope. "The distance."

"Let me see." Charles raised his sniper rifle, aimed at the beast and then dipped his rifle. He slowly raised the end of the barrel. "Trois, quatre, cinque." He sighed in chokes.

"I hate when you do that." Philippe said.

"You shall hate the answer more." Charles took his rifle down and looked at the weather. "The cloud cover is right and the wind is at us, which is good for a gas attack." He touched the pouch that held his gas mask.

"Oui, but the meat … what's the distance?" Philippe didn't like Charles so much. If something had to be done, he always had the reason that it could not be done. For him, if they led an attack Charles would go on about why this was a bad time or that was wrong; he was a naysayer.

"Maybe, forty meters or more." Charles looked just over the sand bags around the trench. "If I was over there," he motioned at the German line. "I'd run my eyes along the ground. Anything different, bang!"

Philippe nearly hit him. His hands were balled up into fists. "Fool, stop your nonsense." He shook his head. "I will go, cut away a large piece, and tie it up." He gathered the rope in his hand. "You will cover me." He tapped Charles on the chest with his forefinger, "and you will not miss."

"Non, of course not, Sargent." He forced a smile.

Philippe took his bandolier off and set it next to his rifle. "We must have the meat."

Charles looked at the men who watched Philippe. "Why not make one of them go?"

"Non, it's for me to do." He said and ran his hands down his jacket. He went to the ladder, lifted his foot and set it on the first step. Then, he didn't move for a few minutes. He bowed his head and prayed.

Charles got a bench and got on it, but did not look over the edge yet. He checked his ammo and then wiped his hands on a chamois cloth. He wiped his trigger finger thoroughly. "I'm ready." He looked at Philippe.

"And I'm not." His foot trembled as he brought it up another step.

Chapter 3: The Horse

Two soldiers nearest him got up and scratched their temples.

"Sargent?" One asked.

"Shh," Philippe said. He got his foot in the next step and waited. Sweat dripped down the sides of his head; the cool air did nothing to stop it. He thought of the fresh grilled horse meat for supper. Perhaps, the priest can bless the meal. He got his foot into the next rung and if he stood, a German sniper would kill him the next second.

He crawled up and laid flat against the ground where bits of dirt came into his nose with each breath he took. The sand bags were a little tough to stay low on and he pulled himself ahead to get over it. Then, his boots came over and that was it. He was in no man's land, the desolate range between enemies where souls are shot or blown out from their human bodies. The air was thick with rot from the dead horse. He turned his head and raised it up just a bit to get a sniff of the air. He squeezed one side of his nostril and blew it clear and then did the other. Then, he wiped his nose and took a very slow whiff of the air. His hand was firmly placed on his gas mask. He choked, but caught his breath, "uh." The smell of a body in decay, a human body, that was, more likely than not, the rider who had been on the horse.

The moment had come. Either he crawled off before dark and got the meat or he let fear push him back to the trench. He looked back and Charles rifle barrel looked past him. He turned back and there, just a few meters ahead of him, was a ragged nest of barbed wire. Much of it was tied or hooked to metal posts that were hammered deep into the ground. He had to make a hole through it for himself and for the meat. Suddenly, he sighed, "damn the luck." The barbed wire was setup so that if you pulled or cut it that portion would likely collapse or snap back on you. "Better to eat rations." He said and looked back at the sand bags. The darkness ate up the ground around him and the sand bags looked flat, beyond his sight. He kind of laughed to himself. He was barely ten meters from their trench.

Men that were seated earlier now stood next to Charles and took bets on the sergeant's likely success. It was quite a brouhaha with all the hushed talk, hands that took or handed over cigarettes or candy for the bet. Every couple of minutes, a soldier got the binoculars and looked for their comrade.

"What's this?" The lieutenant asked.

The men jumped and stood still.

Charles kept his eye on the field, "Sargent Bouchard has gone for some meat."

The lieutenant turned and Father Leauvin walked up to him. "This is Father Leauvin."

The men dipped their heads.

"Allo, men." Father nodded and then looked at Charles. "Where's this man?"

The lieutenant's face warmed at the thought that Sgt. Bouchard was out there. "He's gone into no man's land."

"Oh?" Father Leauvin stepped up to the sand bags, grabbed a board and stood on his tip-toes.

"HEY!" The lieutenant jerked him back, "Father!"

Father and the lieutenant fell back against the dirt wall.

"I … sorry to have grabbed you, but you can't look over." The lieutenant gritted his teeth to stop the mouthful of curse words from coming out. He'd have ripped a man apart with his words for doing something so stupid. "German snipers will shoot you." He drew his hand across his mouth.

"Oh, my goodness." Father got to his feet and dusted himself off. "I'm very sorry."

"I'm sure that the good Lord watches over you." The lieutenant said.

"For most things, but not foolish ones." Father wiped the coolness from his face.

"Indeed," the lieutenant said and then turned his attention to Charles. "How far has he gone?"

Charles whispered and never let his sight move from his gun. "He's at the first wire."

The lieutenant shook his head.

"What's the matter?" Father asked.

"Sargent Bouchard is to be with you, Father. Not going for horse meat in no man's land." The lieutenant paced. "I told him you'd be here this evening."

"Why is it called no man's land?" Father asked and then it hit him as to why. "Sorry, I …"

"No man will live if he goes there." A soldier said.

"Yes, of course." Father bowed his head and brought his hands together. "Dear Lord, there is a man, Sargent Bouchard …"

Philippe reached out with a pair of wire cutters in hand. He knew the setup of the wire, because he was the one who told his men where to put it. He snipped that wire and moved it gently. Then, he snipped another wire and pushed it up. His eyes slowly adjusted to the darkness. The overcast sky did not help, but it would help protect him as it kept a heavy darkness over the land. He pulled himself through wire and crawled a couple of meters. He tilted his head and looked around to get his bearings. There! It was the back leg of the horse, "fifty meters." He scoffed.

Another line of barbed wire with spider hooks. The spider hook was a connector where several strands of wire were hooked to one spot and then bled out from that point. To cut one wire would cause it to coil up sometimes and wrap around you. One of the horse's back legs was caught in a couple of the barbed wires from the spider hooks. Philippe pinched his nose; the smell of the dead rider worsened the closer he got to the horse. He took his scarf from around his neck, rubbed it in the dirt, placed it over his nose and then tied it off to the back of his head. "Damn the smell," he got some dirt in hand and rubbed it on the scarf, better to smell dirt than a corpse.

The horse had pulled two wires down. Philippe needed one more cut to get through the wire here. He edged forward and was a meter from the horses back leg. He held the wire and then snipped it. His grip gave out. The wire recoiled and made a "twang" sound! The noise echoed through no man's land!

A German sniper didn't see the wire move, but he knew the sound of barbed wire when it recoiled. He panned no man's land and slowly looked at every shadow, every outline. He paused at each thing to see if it changed. His fellow soldiers called him the "Fisherman," because he was so patient. He could sit for hours and be fine. His rifle was pointed to the left of Philippe, far to the left. Philippe had some time to cut the meat, tie it off and get back to his line.

Father Leauvin looked through the field binoculars. "Is it normal to take this long?"

Charles looked back for just a second, sighed and then put his eye back to the scope. "Non, but it's not a mission of the sort he's used to."

The lieutenant left some time ago and was upset over the matter, but to have meat was a good thing.

"It's been nearly two hours." Father Leauvin said and looked at the men who waited by small fires.

"It has." Charles said.

"Perhaps, I should go see if he's alright?" Father held his cross and gulped.

Charles didn't look back. "You'll be dead before the first wire."

"Oh," Father pushed the gulp down and gripped his cross tightly.

Charles heard the twang too. He knew if he heard it, then the Germans' heard it. The darkness was hard to overcome even when his eyes adjusted. The trench lights were quite dim. He took his eye from the scope, pressed his fingers hard into his eye sockets and then shook his head. He got his chin rested on the butt of his rifle and his eye lined up with his sights, "ah."

Philippe knew that the Germans were closer to him than the French. He slid closer to the back leg and got his knife out. He studied the edge of the hock and followed it up to the hind quarter. He sighed and shook his head, "the bone." He had nothing to cut through the bone, "damn." He rested his forehead on the ground. If he did it, it would be a bloody mess and the noise to break a bone. Now that he was here, it was the principal of the thing. He wasn't leaving without the meat. He got the rope around the hock and the fetlock. He pulled tightly. The two knots would help to keep it straight when he pulled it back.

He reached up, got his knife at the top of the hind quarter and pushed down hard with the blade. He drew it back and all the way around the hindquarter to get the whole leg. The knife sliced the skin easily; the meat wouldn't be so forgiving. His knife did not have a serrated edge, so to slice through the bone wasn't going to happen. But, he could cut the part between the leg bone and the body. He brought his knife up again and cut hard into the meat. The blade rubbed back and forth against the meat and made a little noise. Most of the blood drained away after the German bomb killed the poor thing. He edged up, but knew that if he got any higher his head or hand would be seen and shot.

The German sniper, The Fisherman, panned the ground. The barrel of his rifle was some twenty meters to the left now of the horse. The horse was about twenty or fewer meters from their lines. He stopped and listened. He waved his hand at a soldier to come to him.

"Ja?" The soldier said under his breath.

"Eine fackel," The Fisherman said.

The soldier crawled away, got a flare gun, checked the chamber and pointed it up. He angled the gun so that it was aimed towards the air above no man's land. "CRACK!" The flare shot up!

Philippe drew his hand back quickly and lay flat against the hock of the horse.

The flare didn't go over him, no … it flew up a few meters from him, but the flare brightened the ground around him.

The Fisherman continued to pan the ground near the horse.

Charles saw just the lump of the horse. "Come back," he said in a hushed tone. "Come back Philippe, this damn horse will get you killed." He looked along the German line and knew it, "le pecheur."

Father Leauvin heard him, "the Fisherman?"

"Oui, a German sniper." Charles said.

"Why that name?" Father asked.

"He's very patient and very good." Charles exhaled slowly.

The flare slowly fell to the ground and a gentle breeze carried it away from Philippe.

"Ah," Father said and pursed his lips.

Philippe looked back at the spider hooks and barbed wire. Maybe it would be best if he quit and left. A German patrol would have him if they came. His heart beat harder against his chest so much so that it thumped the ground and yelled, "RUN!" He took a breath, held it and then let it out slowly. He was no amateur, not fresh meat on the field. He survived many runs against the Germans.

He got his hand back to the cut and drew his knife back fast, then again and again until he hit the bone. He couldn't reach it with one hand. He had to edge up and to the side. But, he might be seen, "tant pis." He pushed his feet against the dirt and edged up. He got his other hand in the meat, found the bone and brought his knife in. It was nearly broken through from the bomb. He cut quickly and sweat dripped into his eyes where it stung. His breath gave short bursts of white clouds every time he exhaled now that the cooler air came in this late night. The knife plunged! He was through. Now, to cut the bottom and leave, all he had to do was slice a few more times.

The Fisherman's rifle was pointed just to the side of the horse. He paused. "Eine fackel."

The soldier loaded another flare, aimed up and shot, "CRACK!" The flare popped and no man's land was alight.

Philippe couldn't stop now. He was nearly through the leg. He had to move the hock forward to get the cut done, but he knew someone might see it. He shook his head and moved the hock.

The Fisherman aimed at the horse and saw the horse's rump lower. "Frederick."

"Ja?"

"Dem pferd," he said and sharpened his aim.

Frederick nodded and went to his men. The men got up and got their rifles in position.

Philippe didn't look at the flare. It was nearly to the ground. The light from it crawled across everything and followed its life source to its death. It was dark again. He turned and had the other end of the rope firmly in hand. His boots were at the back of the horse, so he pushed off.

"BANG!" The Fisherman shot! The bullet went right through the hock and just missed Philippe's head!

Charles moved his aim. When he saw the muzzle flash, he'd have the shooter.

"Oh Lord," Father said and looked at the men who got to their feet.

The German's had the ground covered. Their machine gunner glared through his aiming stakes.

Philippe low crawled quickly back through the barbed wire and past the spider hooks. His boot caught a piece of wire and held him!

"FEUER!" The Germans' shot at anything.

Charles shot at a couple of muzzle flashes, but the bullets hit the Germans berm.

The bullets from the German line blasted through the horse and chipped away at the ground! Bits of dirt and chunks of horse meat flew into the air!

Philippe was through the second line of wire and wiped at his face. The dark drool that slid down the side of his face was blood from a barb that sliced him. He threw his elbows out, dug in, and then drew his left elbow back, then his right elbow, then left! His face slid along the ground.

The Fisherman studied the barbed wire near the spider hooks. He followed the possible trail back to the French line. "Yes, you're headed back."

The French shot back, but the lieutenant made them stop to conserve ammunition. Also, he didn't want them to shoot his sergeant.

The Germans stopped shooting.

Smoke from the gunfire rose up from both lines along no man's land.

Philippe was nearly back to the French lines. It was easy to get turned around in no man's land and end up at the wrong trench.

The Fisherman was at the sand bags that separated no man's land from the French trenches. He settled on a spot, sighed and then aimed.

Philippe saw the sand bags and heaved in breaths. He lay still for a moment. Fear and anxiety made his heart beat at a fierce pace! He wiped his brow and swallowed the dryness of his mouth hard. He checked the rope. Now was not the time to have the rope come up short as he crossed the sand bags. There was plenty of rope left.

The Fisherman wondered what they were doing by the horse. Perhaps, to get their man back? He looked quickly at the dead rider who lay partially across a broken branch, "nein." He checked his target.

Philippe saw the tip of Charles's rifle. The place he had to crawl back over was a meter or two ahead of him. He sighed. "Je commence." He edged up and crawled on. Anyone else might think to get up and run, but that was the surest way to be shot in the back.

Now, he was at the sand bags. Some of the clouds had cleared and the partial moon lit up the ground around him, "tant pis or so much the worse." It was now. He tightened his grip on the rope. He stretched his legs and shook his hands. He whispered, "This meat had better taste like filet mignon after this sacrifice." Then, he uttered the password. "Lunaire"

Charles leaned closer to the sandbags, "oui, come."

Philippe dug his foot in and thrust himself forward!

The Fisherman studied the spot to the right of where Philippe crawled to safety. Then, he saw the shadow of something right in front of the sand bags! He aimed!

Philippe went headfirst over the bags and his boot went up!

"BANG!" The bullet hit the heel of Philippe's boot!

"AH!" He fell into the trench and onto Father Leauvin!

"My God!" Father tried to stop his fall, but they both fell to the ground.

"Mon pied!" He let the rope go and looked at his boot. "AH!" The bullet ripped through the heel, but that was it. "Dieu merci, merci beaucoup!" He leaned back and raised his hands. "Yes."

"Yes, thank God." Father said and helped him up.

Charles eased down and looked him over. "You have the meat then?"

Philippe tapped Charles shoulder, "Quickly!" They pulled the rope and the hock came.

The Fisherman saw the horse move again. He shook his head. "They were after the meat." He looked at Frederick. "We blew the damn beast up … you should have thought to get it."

"I wasn't hungry." Frederick said.

The Fisherman smacked him on his helmet. "And now?" He climbed down and set his rifle down.

Philippe saw the dark mass slide towards them and then stop. Charles got the rope and pulled. The hock flipped up and over!

"All that for some meat?" Father asked.

"Oui, all that." Philippe said.

Charles looked at Father, "Sargent Bouchard, je te present Father Leauvin."

Philippe and Father nodded at each other.

Philippe looked at the men as cigarettes and candy changed hands. "Some of that better come my way." He looked at Father, "it's only fair." He wiped his face. "Are you hungry, Father?"

"After all that with the horse, of course." Father said.

Chapter 4: The Enemy

Father let the men go at the first cuts of meat from the horse. They weren't large cuts, but enough so that the men got to taste and have a chew. Luckily, the meat hadn't turned yet. The cool air helped to keep the meat semi-fresh.

"Father?" Philippe asked. "I'm afraid there are no forks."

"Yes, thank you." He got it. "I'm fine to eat with my hands." He tore a bite from the meat.

"So, you'll show me the place?" Father asked and wondered about the time. It had to be after midnight.

"Yes, as it's quiet, I'm going to clean up and rest some." He dipped his helmet at Father, "good night, Father."

"Good night," Father smiled.

Philippe disappeared into the shadows.

Father chewed hard on the meat and the lieutenant walked up. "Ah, so you've had some horse."

"Yes, and some rest after." He dipped his head. "Good night, Lieutenant."

"Father."

Father chewed up the last piece and walked to his quarters. His quarters were a small dugout with a canvas cover. The smell of raw dirt and gun powder made his nose itch. He checked his camera and then knelt for prayers. "Dear Lord, thank you that I've made the journey here. To serve you and help these men," his hands tightened. "And to find my way among them for my own sake, my soul's sake ... amen."

The early morning air drifted across no man's land towards the French trenches; some men clutched their gas masks. They wondered if the Germans might launch a chemical attack; they had happened often enough and the Germans hoped that the use of the gas would break the spirit of the French and bring an early victory.

The lieutenant walked along some busted wood planks to keep his boots out of the mud. By mid-June, there were some hard thunderstorms; the trenches filled with water easily and the trenches turned into a swamp.

The lieutenant held a gas mask in his hand and had one on his hip along with his pistol. "Father?" He looked into the dugout where Father Leauvin rested.

"Yes," he took some water from the basin and washed his face. "Please," he motioned for the lieutenant to come in.

"Good morning, have you slept well?" The lieutenant rubbed his chin whiskers.
He shrugged his shoulders, "as well as is possible here."

He dried his face, got his collar and put it in place. Then, he noticed a canvas bag in the lieutenant's hand.

"Ah, a gas mask." He handed it to Father. "It's fine for mustard gas, but …" He looked around.

"But?" He took the mask.
"It's not useful for chlorine gas." He stepped up to Father so that his voice would not carry. "We won't have replacements until July."

"For what?"

"For a mask that will filter out the chlorine." He cleared his throat. "Diphosgene smells like musty hay sometimes, so don't take another breath until you've got your mask on … oh, and be sure to get away from it." He put his finger tips on his nose, pinched it shut and grinned.

Father gulped. "I see, but you said this particular mask does not work for chlorine gas?"

His grin faded. "Yes, but it's better than nothing." The lieutenant showed him how to use the mask and Father was rather clumsy with the straps, but managed it after repeated tries. "Good, that's it then."

"We hope." He grinned. "Thank you, Lieutenant."

"Quite welcome, Sargent Bouchard will be along soon." He went to the trench and turned. "I've some canned fruit … if you like?"

Father thought for a moment, "No, thank you."

The lieutenant nodded and went back to the command tent.

"Father," Philippe walked in. "See you've got your mask." He laughed. "The things are useless against the gas ghost."

"Ah, yes, the lieutenant told me that the mask won't filter the chlorine." Father checked himself over.

"Better than nothing." Philippe said and brought his rifle around.

"He said that too." Father laughed.

"Are you hungry?"

"Not really, I … is it possible to walk the trench now?" Father went to Philippe, "to see the men."

"Of course," Philippe stepped out and into the trench. "Your cloth may be too long for the mud."

"I'm fine." Father walked out, got his hand tight around his cassock and pulled it up.

The few boards that were placed in the trench were not enough to keep anyone from the mud; you were surrounded by it. The smell of raw dirt, exposed dead roots and the bugs made Father's nose twitch.

"It's quite a different smell." Father rubbed his nose.

"Dirt, piss and …" Philippe stopped himself. "Sorry, Father."

"No, it's alright. I've heard …" His voice trailed off.

"Worse?" Philippe got a cigarette and lit it. "You surprise me, Father."

"I have yet to surprise myself, Sargent." Father stumbled on some mud caked up around the end of the board where the men scraped it off their boots.

"It's fine to call me, Philippe." He said and moved his cigarette around as he talked: up for happiness, down for unpleasantness and back and forth in the middle for just conversation; he moved it precisely.

"I'd say to call me, Robert." He smiled, "but the order wouldn't allow for it." He stumbled and fell against the wall of the trench. "I'm usually much more balanced."

"You'll learn soon enough." Philippe helped him up.

"So, where are we headed?"

Philippe drew in the last of the cigarette, let it fall to the ground and then crushed it with his boot. "First, to the command tent." He pointed up the path. "Then, we'll go round and meet with the men."

"Is there a chance of an attack?" Father tried to peer over the sand bags of dirt.

"Hey!" Philippe grabbed at his shirt. "You'll get shot."

"Ah, sorry. I forgot that." Father shook his head. "Stupid of me."

"Don't forget again, Father or a German sniper will remind you." Philippe sighed hard.

They walked past soldiers who cleaned their guns or checked their gas masks. Most nodded and were courteous. Some forced a grin and had a worrisome look on their face. Death was around them every day, but to have a priest in the trench, sometimes, added up to last rights, not a blessing.

Father said, "allo" often, but very few said anything. Most of the men nodded at him or said, "Father."

Philippe stopped at the entrance to the command tent. A couple of men stood and looked at a map. The lieutenant looked up.

"Ah, Father, good morning." He smiled heartily.

"Yes, good morning." Father dipped his head.

"So, Sgt. Bouchard's showing you around." He looked around the tent. "Might be best if you kept a helmet with you."

"Oh?"

"Bombings happen with chunks of dirt and metal thrown in the air." He got a helmet from a large green trunk. "Here you are."

"May I prefer to wear it as needed?" Father got the helmet and left it in hand at his side.

"Uh," the lieutenant thought for a moment, "yes, that's fine ... for the moment."

"What are you doing?" Father looked the map over.

"We're updating our maps, positions of German gun placements, trenches, and our lines." He tapped the map. "Get Legume to go with …"

"Lieutenant," Sgt. Bouchard saluted.

"Ah, Sgt. Bouchard." The Lieutenant saluted him. "What is it then?"

"May I suggest, Private Dussier?" Sgt. Bouchard looked over the map, "He's very fast and his vision is the best, very sharp."

"Good, that's it then." The lieutenant looked at the map.

"Sir, if our men go here, they can make their way along these bomb craters." Bouchard followed a makeshift line, "and from this side, the rising sun will be in the Germans' eyes."

"Bouchard, that's very good." The lieutenant looked at a runner. "Go, tell Legume and Dussier to make the most of their mission."

"Sir!" The short soldier saluted, got to the entrance and vanished.

"You see the German placements haven't moved very much. Von Falkenhayns judgement …"

"Sorry?" Father said and looked at Sgt. Bouchard.

"Von Falkenhayns is the German General who planned the attack on Verdun." The lieutenant said. "He planned to bleed France white." The lieutenant grinned. "We were so much stronger than he knew and it cost them dearly."

"It did, sir." Sgt. Bouchard said.

"Because of the casualties?" Father asked.

"Theirs and ours, but the former was far worse than Falkenhayns imagined." The lieutenant sighed and nodded, "We were stronger, more courageous."

"Ah, we are French." Father said.

"Indeed," the lieutenant pointed at the map. "They came across our border and thought to sack our forts, draw us into a battle to the end of our last man, but no." Pride swelled up inside him. Even Philippe felt it. "The men fought and fought well."

"The Lord's blessings … thank God." Father said.

The lieutenant was taken for a moment and then caught his breath, "Yes, thank God."

"And the men," Sgt. Bouchard said.

"Sorry, of course, the men sacrificed ultimately." There was an uncomfortable moment and silence took the place of words. Father drew his hand along the map and wondered what to say to those whose faith was in question. He hadn't seen the bodies of men killed in no man's land or anywhere else. The bishop warned him and, now, he knew that the awkwardness was because of him. "So, we were to visit the men?"

"Yes, Father." Sgt. Bouchard saluted the lieutenant. "Sir."

"The lieutenant saluted, "bon chance, Father." A funny thing to say.

"Thank you, Lieutenant." Father walked out and stood.

Philippe walked past and Father followed.

"I can imagine that it's hard to hold onto faith or God in a place like this." Father held his cross.

Philippe stopped and turned to him. "To be honest," he said and waited.

"Yes, please."

"When you step past a dead man and then realize that you've stepped on some of his guts … this is the test that questions God's work and we think on our faith." Philippe and Father locked eyes. The seconds that passed felt like minutes. Then, Philippe cleared his throat, got a cigarette and lit up. "Excuse me, Father. I don't mean to speak ill of …"

"It's … I understand." Father said and thought about the girl who waved to him as he stood on the steps to the church. "It's shameful that the world, the people of this world don't strive for something more." He let loose of his cross, put his hands to his back and held the helmet with both hands. "When we are confronted, we fight for our beliefs, fight for our land …"

"Fight for our souls." Philippe said and blew a puff of smoke up. "Come on."

They walked further down the trench. "How far does this trench go?"

"A kilometer or so."

"Really, my goodness." Father got hold of the leather strap of the helmet and put it on.

"Here," Philippe said and helped him with it.

"Thank you," Father pushed the front up enough to see clearly.

"Charles," Philippe dipped his head at the man who was their best sniper.

"Allo," he looked at the priest. "Father."

"Allo, Charles?" They shook.

"Sgt. Tourmet," he said and held his rifle across his chest. "So, you're walking the trench?"

"Yes, to show him and to say hello to the men." Philippe looked ahead.

Charles's brows went up. "I'm sure they are ready to visit."

"You are a sniper?" Father asked.

"Oui, the best of the entire French Army." He held up his rifle. "I've killed …"

Philippe's eyes got big and he shook his head gently.

"Ah, well it's not that important." Charles forced himself to smile.

Father smiled politely. "I'm happy you're on our side."

"The Germans not so much." Charles said.

"We should get on." Philippe said.

Charles and Philippe nodded at each other.

Father and Philippe stopped and visited with several more men; Private Lachance who was Catholic and prayed with Father. Private Sout was very quiet and Father got or heard all of five words, "happy to do my duty," from the young man.

They reached the end of the trench by mid-day and had some water. Philippe looked at the sandbags and a tunnel. "This goes to a hiding place and then to another trench."

"It's quite a lot to take in."

"Wait till they attack." Philippe said. "There's a rumor that the German's want to break the stalemate."

"I see."

"They may launch a large attack soon." He looked at his rifle. "You'll have plenty to pray for."

"I'm here for more than that, Sargent." Father said and looked at the tunnel. "Where are the German lines?"

Philippe looked at a ladder and pondered. He tipped his helmet up. "See for yourself, but keep your head low."

"I thought you said that a sniper …"

"Oui, a sniper, but here there is a berm around you. Our machine gunners use this position to set up in." He moved the ladder. "You can see the German line as the ground beyond the berm is nearly flat."

Father gulped and he scratched his arm, but all of his skin itched and bubbled up with goosebumps. "Are you sure?"

"Yes, Father." He looked up. "I'll go first to show you how."

"Perhaps, we should get back?" Father wiped the sweat from his brow.

"Father, you must work on your fear." Philippe said and was a little annoyed with all that he'd been through. He thought on the men who'd been destroyed in no man's land. "Have faith."

Father cleared his throat, "of course."

"So, one step up -- you see the berm's top. Do not get your head higher than here." Philippe pointed at the top of the berm. "Look ahead, through the gunner's position," he pointed. "You'll see the German flag and they are just ahead of it." He spat.

"I understand."

Philippe got down and held his hand out to usher Father onto the ladder.

"Yes, alright then." Father got his foot on the first rung and then he stepped up. His muddy shoe gave out and slipped off! "Ah!"

"Easy Father, it's just the mud from your shoe." Philippe held the ladder.

"Yes, just mud." He tried to control the trembling that ate up his arms and legs. Slowly, he edged his foot back onto the rung, then another and up he went. His head was close to the top of the sandbags and Philippe pulled at Father's coat.

"Now, look across no man's land." He held onto Father's coat and was ready to pull him down.

Father peered through the gunner's position and through wooden stakes on either side. "What are the wooden stakes for?"

"Limiting stakes, they stop the gunner from going too far to the left or right." Philippe knew that the Germans watched them and they'd see a soldier in the gunner spot. "Have you seen enough?"

"I think so. The German flag looks so close to here." Father edged back, his head went up and over the sandbag!

"BANG!" A shot rang out! "CLANG!" It ricocheted off of Father's helmet!

Father's head jerked back and he fell to the mud! "I'm shot! I'm shot!"

Philippe looked at him and then at his helmet, "no, you're okay Father, it ricocheted off your helmet."

"Are you sure!" He ran his hands all over the helmet, tore it from his head and pressed his fingers against the sore spot on his scalp. "Blood, is there blood?"

"No, Father, no blood." Philippe fought his urge to laugh. He wondered if Father had crapped or pissed himself. He wanted to tell the Fisherman that he'd nearly killed a priest.

Father did his best to get ahold of himself. His hands, arms and legs shook. "My God," he said and got his cross in hand. "I'm a priest." He tried to get to his feet, but sat back down.

"Yes, but they don't see that from their side." Philippe could stop it no longer; he laughed.

"What's so funny?" Father's face went from ghost white to fire engine red in less than a second. "Excuse me, Sgt. Bouchard." He got to his feet with a firm grip on the ladder.

"Sorry, but your face when you came down." Philippe bent over and laughed heartily.

Some soldiers came up and looked them over. One looked at Father, "the Fisherman?"

"Who cares!" Father yelped. "I *was* nearly killed." He pulled at his cassock and it was muddy.

"We have all been nearly killed, Father." The Soldier said. "Some have been killed. You were lucky."

Father got his composure, "The enemy should be told that I'm a priest and not a target."

"And the rest of us?" The very young man asked.

Father looked at Philippe and then the soldiers. "I'm so sorry." He swallowed hard to get his bearings. "I was frightened by the bullet."

"You're alright Father." Philippe patted Father's back. "The enemy will know you soon enough."

Chapter 5: Camaraderie

End of June 1916, Verdun

The quiet unsettled the men. Father was unsettled too; it was only a week after the Fisherman bounced a bullet off of his helmet. Father still had the helmet and refused to relinquish it for a new one. The men signed around the bullet mark with funny sayings, "a good miss!" and "poor helmet, rich priest." Father felt that the helmet was his good luck charm or, more so, a blessing from the Lord.

Rumors of a major offensive swirled around the men in hushed conversations. The lieutenant waited on word from command and hoped to have some notice before they were attacked. Scouts kept a watchful eye and held their whistles close. Bombardments usually started an offensive to soften the line and then they were followed by German troops that attacked en masse. That evening, it *was* quiet.

Father prayed and then cleaned his camera. He eyed the lens and wiped it with a cloth; the cloth wasn't as clean as he'd like, but it would do. So far, he took pictures of the trenches; the vast network of ditches that were as deep as a man's head and meandered like a lazy stream across the countryside of France.

Philippe stopped, "There may be an offensive soon."

"Yes, I heard." He moved the pictures so that Philippe saw them.

"Ah, your photos have come out well." He said, stepped under the cover and into the dugout.

"Yes, I'm pleased." Father wiped the sides of the camera and then gently touched around the small crank.

"It's a French Camera?" Philippe looked at a picture of a trench where some of the men stood just inches above the mud on a broken pallet.

"No, a gift from my parents … it was made in the Etats Unis." He held it up. "It's very sturdy with precise optics … a Tourist Multiple."

Philippe looked it over, "My hands are quite dirty."

Father smiled, "it's a thirty-five-millimeter camera."

"The pictures are quite nice." Philippe put a picture of another trench with no one in it next to the one with the soldiers. "This one of just the trench is haunting."

"Because there are no soldiers?" Father turned and looked it over.

"Yes, it's empty of life." Philippe said. "A scar that never sees the stitch and so it can never close."

Father sighed politely and understood Philippe's take on the photo. "For me, I see it as peace."

"Peace?" Philippe moved his helmet back to let the heat off his scalp.

"Yes, the men are home and the trench is abandoned." Father moved his fingers gently over the faces of the men in the other photo. "I pray for an empty trench."

Philippe tried not to laugh. "When the offensive begins, they will empty." He pulled his helmet down and walked out. "It may be best for you to stay near the command tent."

"For me, but not for the men." Father said, stood and dipped his head at Philippe.

"As you like, I'll come to you if an attack begins this night. If not, then I'll be here in the morning." Philippe nodded and left.

Father forced himself to smile, but the notion of an impending attack unsettled his nerves. Anxiety pulsed through his veins with each beat of his heart. If he felt that rush of worry and fear, then the men must feel some sort of it. He got his helmet on, set his camera down and went out.

"Raphael," he nodded at the soldier who sat with a few other men. Some smoked, others ate what little they had to eat, and one played a flute softly.

"The music is quite nice." Father stood to the side.

Two soldiers passed and one carried a machine gun; the other carried several belts of ammunition.

Father whispered to a man next to him. "Yann, he's quite good."

"Yes, father." Yann said and bit at his lip. "Later, perhaps you'll have some time for a prayer?"

"Of course," Father said.

The man finished his soft tune and set the flute aside for hot tea.

"So, father … will this be your first time in an attack?" Raphael asked.

Yann's face warmed and the glow from the oil lamp showed that his cheeks went from yellow to red. "Must you ask such a thing?" He snapped.

"It's alright, Yann." Father said. "I shall do as any man when the time comes." He nodded at Raphael, "drink tea and then take cover."

The men chuckled.

Raphael shook his head, "only with your lucky helmet on."

The men laughed and did not mind the noise.

Father nodded at each of them, "I shall pray for all of you."

The lightened expressions of the men drooped at the idea that Father would pray for them. Some of them were glad to know it, but the truth was that his words made the thought of death real before it had reached them.

Father realized his words upset them, "to have tea."

The men knew why he said what he said and a few chuckles came through the thick air. Father walked away, further along the trench where the moonlight was all there was for portions of the trench. Oil lamps were in short supply and hung forty or more meters apart.

Father stopped at a man who looked through field binoculars. "Can you see anything in this darkness?" His anxiety edged up at the sight of someone looking for something, an attack.

"What a stupid thing to ask." The soldier said and then took his gaze from the binoculars. "Ah, Father, I'm so sorry."

Father looked at him and smiled. "It's me, it was stupid to ask."

"In the trench, so many things are new and curious to you." The soldier took a half-smoked cigarette from his pocket. "How are you?"

Father was terrified and moved his shaking hands to his back where he clasped them together so that they could comfort each other. "Nervous."

The soldier lit his cigarette and drew in a deep breath. "Well, there is first the shock that you really are under attack." He smiled and held the smoke in for a moment. "Then, there is the second thing that you wish you were anywhere but here."

Father chuckled, "I told the men that I'd have tea and then take cover when the attack came."

The soldier shook his head. "Perhaps, that's better to enjoy something good before …"

"Yes?" Father raised his brow and then realized that he just asked another stupid thing.

The man looked away.

Father thought and then said, "Did you have any of the horse?"

"Horse?" The soldier looked Father over and then sniffed the air between them. Had Father been drinking?

"The meat …" Father said.

"Ah, oui … yes, just enough to taste it." The soldier said.

Father smiled, "What's your name?" He looked at the man's jacket, but there wasn't any indication of a name tag. "I'm sorry I don't recall."

"What will it matter?" The soldier said, rubbed the burning ash from his cigarette and put it in his pocket. He seemed indignant, but not towards Father. "Sorry Father, but what's a name to a German bullet, nothing."

Father put his hand on the man's shoulder. "Your name matters to your friends. It matters to your parents, your family and it matters to me and to God."

The soldier pursed his lips, stood straight, extended his hand and locked eyes with Father. "Je m'appelle Michael Souleur."

"Father Leauvin." He smiled.

"I must get back to my watch." Pvt. Souleur said.

"Nice to meet you," Father said.

"And you," Pvt. Souleur said and smiled back. Then, he returned his eyes to the small round metal rings of the binoculars.

Father walked away and whispered a prayer for Pvt. Souleur, "Amen."

No attack last night and Philippe tapped on a wood post that held up the makeshift cover over Father's cot and desk. The sun was just above the horizon and fought a haze that hung over no mans land.

"I'm up." Father stood.

Philippe moved the tattered cloth to the side and stepped in. "Some coffee?"

"Yes," they walked towards the command tent.

The lieutenant drank his coffee and looked at Father. "Father, good morning."

Several other soldiers stood nearby.

"Good morning, Lieutenant." Father pointed at the pot, "may I?"
"Of course," the lieutenant said. "How are your pictures coming?"

"Ah, well …" awkwardness overcame him. He wasn't there just to take pictures. "They are quite nice. I hope to get some of the battlefield."

A sudden and overwhelming silence took control of the soldiers. Philippe choked, but caught his breath. To take any pictures of the battlefield meant that Philippe would go with Father into no man's land. "Father, to do so … to take pictures in no man's land is …" Philippe blurted out.

The lieutenant cleared his throat and had his coffee close, over his heart. "I don't believe I can allow myself to put you in such grave danger."

"Ah, I'm sorry." Father said and then thought about it.

A few chuckles slipped past pressed lips.

The lieutenant set his coffee down. "Father, we are always fighting." He looked at the map on the table and put his index on a spot just east of Verdun. "German forces are amassing here. Austro-Hungarian here." He moved his finger. "We are at war." He tried to smile so that his words were not harsh. "You ask to go into the open; into the area between us and our enemy … I cannot allow it."

"Surely," Father said.

"No, it's not possible." The lieutenant said and looked at Philippe. "Father, do you know why you were asked to come this many years on to Verdun?"

"Yes, as a priest necessary to the will of God for the men." Father said plainly.

"Was it then the will of God that Father Montage be killed for your arrival?" The lieutenant pursed his lips hard. "I'm sorry, but the only times when any of my men are in no man's land are to save a man or charge the Germans." He picked up his coffee and sipped.

Father's throat felt swollen. "Sorry, I … I didn't mean to."

"It's alright, Father. I know now you understand to keep your lucky helmet close." The lieutenant said, set his coffee down and then lifted the pot. "Some more coffee?"

Near supper time, Father and Philippe walked the trench some distance from the command tent.
"You seem distant Father." Philippe stopped.

Father stopped and turned to face no man's land. "I feel that my … part of my wish was realized and then the worst part of it was realized only after the lieutenant spoke."

"Father, surely you can't imagine a walk in no man's land. The barbed wire, the possibility of gas drifting there and the Fisherman."

"The Fisherman?"

"The German sniper whose patience is profound and whose bullet gave you a headache." Philippe looked at the desolate divide between them and the German line. "One man wandering out there. And for what? A picture?" He shook his head hard. "It's likely the offensive we've heard of will begin soon." He touched his gas mask. "I see you don't have it."

Father looked at Philippe and then at his hip. "No, I … I forgot it."

"You've not seen what the gas does to a person." Philippe turned. "I have it here for you." He held up Father's gas mask.

"You're a very good soldier." Father said and got the mask from him.

"I am alive." Philippe turned back the way that they came. "We should get back."

"Yes," Father turned and then stopped. He turned his head cockeyed. "You hear that?"

Philippe hunched down. Then, he grabbed Father by the collar and jerked him to the ground! "GET DOWN!"

Chapter 6: The Attack on the Monster's Back

Bombs whistled through the air! BOOM! Dirt, rock and debris blasted up and around them! The ground shook so hard that Father dropped his gas mask.

"We must get back!" Philippe grabbed Father's gas mask and shoved it into Father's hand. He turned and pulled Father along. "C'mon!"

The whistling was unmistakable, BOOM! The ground shook and dirt fell on their helmets.

"My God," Father yelped.

BOOM! BOOM! BOOM! Large plumes of white smoke blew up into the darkened sky!

Philippe and Father fell into the mud.

A man just up from them had his gas mask on and tapped it with his fingers; then, he pointed at them.

"Gas!" Philippe held his breath, put his mask on and then sealed it. His voice was muffled by the mask as he yelled at Father, "Your mask!"

Father clumsily pulled the mask out. His hand trembled so badly that he couldn't get it right in his hands. Philippe jerked Father's helmet off, grabbed his gas mask and put it on him. Then, he motioned for him to press it tightly against his face and breathe. The large ovals in the mask for his eyes sunk down to his nose.

"Breathe!" Philippe yelled and pulled Father's mask up so that his eyes were lined up with the oval cups.

Dirt and shrapnel flew all around them!

Father's eyes were a ghostly gray and what part of his face was visible was pale and near death.

"You are okay!" Philippe got Father's helmet and handed it to him. "Put it on!"

Father got his senses back, some of them, and put his helmet back on. Then, he pulled the strap under his chin and nodded at Philippe.

BOOM! A line of barbed wire and spider connectors were blown apart! The wires flew up and then back towards the French lines. BOOM!

Another explosion blasted away at sand bags some distance behind Father and Philippe; the blasts collapsed a large wall of the trench and Philippe watched in horror as two soldiers, Yann perhaps was one, were swallowed whole by a mouth made of mud, piss, blood and crap.

A soft cloud seeped over the freshly vomited piles of dirt and bodies. The gaseous tentacles of phosgene gas slowly pulled itself along the barren ground into the trench.

BOOM!

Bombs hit in no man's land! Bombs hit right at the crest of the trench! Bombs hit behind the trench and the gas clouds grew thicker and thicker!

The French artillery returned fire and their bombs whistled past the men!

"FATHER! MOVE!" Philippe yelled, grabbed Father's arm and pulled him along. They rushed down the trench to the command center, a turn here and a turn there, then BOOM!

Bomb after bomb shook the earth so hard that Father and Philippe fell again and again.

"Damn Germans!" Philippe shouted. They got up and soft, gray clouds drifted across the trench.

Father looked towards the command tent, "Dear Lord." A man gripped his throat and gasped for air! Father stumbled over wood planks and chunks of dirt to get to the man.

Philippe saw Father and ran after him!

"Hold on!" Father shouted. Thick spit stuck to the man's mouth like a spider's web to a house. "Hold on, just …" Father helped him get his gas mask on and saw that his eyes were closed.

BOOM! This time the blasts were different. The explosions were louder and the blasts roared through the ground!

"We must get him to the medics!" Philippe and Father lifted the man and dragged him away.

BOOM! They fell into the mud. They picked the man up again and then carried him off.

Philippe knew the German's changed their bombs. "High explosive bombs now!"

"What?" Father shouted, tripped and fell. "Please Lord, help me to find my footing."

"After gas bombs, they change to high explosive!" Philippe looked ahead through lenses that had mud speckled over them. Everything was dark and smoked covered.

A solider ran right into them! "Sgt. Bouchard!"

"Calm down," Philippe said and rolled his eyes.

"The lieutenant orders you to the command tent!" The soldier lost his footing.

Several whistling sounds ripped the air to pieces!

"GET DOWN!" Philippe yelled.

Father tried to help the choking man to the ground, but Philippe shoved them down! BOOM! BOOM! BOOM! BOOM! Dirt and shrapnel lashed out at everything in their path.

The flashes of light fractured into a kaleidoscope against the white clouds. The high explosives blasted monstrous craters out of the ground; the earth cringed with every hit; her soul was ripped apart.

Men cowered in the shadows and fought to catch their breath. The masked figurines were lost in the darkness and their souls cried to get free from their human cage.

"We must get moving!" Philippe shouted.

Father got to his feet and lifted the man, but he was a ragdoll. The man's limbs flopped around and slipped right through Father's hands. "What's happened!"

BOOM! Boom! The bombing tapered off.

Philippe let go of his comrade and gently shook his head at Father.

Father knelt, took the man's hand and spoke the last rites.

Philippe tapped Father's shoulder, "He's dead!"

"Not yet," Father kept on and put his ear to the man's mask.

Philippe looked around to get some idea of where they were. A lantern glowed in the darkness maybe twenty or more meters from them.

BOOM! The ground shook so hard that Philippe fell against the dirt wall.

They left the man and, finally, got to the command tent. One dirt wall had collapsed and covered much of the supplies. Two soldiers used their shovels to dig away at the dirt heap.

Philippe heard the whistling trails of bombs freshly shot from the German's guns. They landed farther away now and, he wondered, were infantry coming? "Have we any word on German infantry?"

Everyone was foreign to each other; the gas mask, with their odd, large oval eye slots, gave the appearance of beings from another world who spoke in muffled words.

The lieutenant did not have his helmet on and had a bloody cut across the side of his head. "No, but if they've shifted their fire, then it's probable." He wiped at the blood and dirt that mashed into a kind of red clay. "Bouchard," he got his map back on the table.

The bombing continued but had shifted up the line.

"Go down the line and see if any of our machine guns are still up!" He motioned for two other soldiers to go too. "You two go down the line. Check for wounded too!"

The two men left to check for wounded. Philippe left to check the machine guns.

Father looked around at the men and the objects that littered the room. It was so foreign to him that he thought he was at a stage show until another bomb hit and shook the ground! "What … will there be an attack? I … I mean an infantry attack?"

"It's likely." The lieutenant got his bearings and looked the map over. "They blew the wire in many places. We must get ready." He rubbed the cut to his head. "My helmet?" He looked around.

A runner burst around the corner and handed a note to the lieutenant.

The lieutenant read the note and then ran his fingers along the map's line between them and the Germans. "The gas and HE were to soften us up, kill as many as possible." He got his whistle out and looked it over. "They want us to prepare to attack." His helmet was just there by the wall and the runner handed it to him.

"That's madness." Father said. "You can't see a thing and what about the wounded?"

"Madness is a part of war, Father." The lieutenant fixed his helmet back on his head, scribbled something on a paper, and then handed it to the runner. "In this madness, we must find ourselves and focus on the task at hand."

The runner took off!

The lieutenant tapped the soldier who dug at the dirt covered supplies. "Get anyone that can walk and shoot, tell them to take positions and be ready for no man's land."

"Sir!" The soldier left and, now, it was just Father and the lieutenant.

"If you wish to take any pictures," he turned the lamp up. "Now, is the time."

Father was dumbfounded and didn't know what to think. Then, he nodded and went to his dugout. The top was blown off, but the table and cot were okay. He got his camera from under a large crate and came back. The oil lamp was bright enough, but to get the camera right with the gas mask on was going to be very hard. After a few changes, he took a picture of the lieutenant looking at the map and then a couple of the command tent.

"Will they develop?" The lieutenant asked.

"I don't know."

Philippe rounded the corner, "Sir, two machine gun positions survived, but one of the gunners is dead."

"We have men coming from another regiment." He went to the trench and looked both ways. "We are going to attack. I want ..." The lieutenant looked up and then at Philippe. "Who's the young man ... Chauvin?"

"Yann Chauvin, he's dead sir ... buried under ...." Philippe looked at Father and then at the lieutenant.

"Find a man to take his position. They will come over with us and set up at the far end for suppression fire." The lieutenant looked at his map. "Twenty minutes, and where's my report on the wounded!"

A soldier ducked in, "Sir, we have some ten dead and, maybe, twenty or more wounded."

"Damn the luck," he turned away from them. "There will be reinforcements soon."

A strong wind shook the tent covers.

The lieutenant stepped back to the trench. "Thank God, the wind."

Philippe looked at Father, "It will push out the gas and the smoke."

Father nodded, "but the German infantry …"

"They will attack soon." Philippe said. "We will meet them in no man's land."

Wounded were taken away; the dead were lined up and covered some distance from the trenches. Hours passed and the lieutenant had no word from HQ to go forward with the attack. The reinforcements, fifty or more soldiers, lined up along the trench and all wore their gas mask. The lieutenant let his men break to rest, one up and one down. Exhaustion chewed on the men and ate up what little energy they had left. It was early morning now.

The glare from the sun through the mist was a shattered orange. Dirt ridden men sighed heavily to push away the weight of exhaustion that sat on their shoulders. Sgt. Bouchard wondered about life elsewhere and peered through the field binoculars; he hoped the Germans would come and not the other way around.

Father spoke with some men and prayed. He had his bible and his camera.

The sergeants were ready with their whistles; they'd have to lift their gas mask and blow quickly.

The toxic air that crept across their trench like a filthy beast intent on killing or maiming for no other reason than to have death in its company was gone.

They got the "all clear" to remove their gas mask; five hours was a long time to have your face covered with raw rubber. But, the new threat was upon them.

They *were* going to attack the German lines. Miles of barbed wire and spider connectors were torn up and thrown all over. So, the men would have to figure out the terrain as they ran across it. Then, they had to shoot at the enemy while being shot at. The "Fisherman" had his sniper rifle ready and there was little need to be patient when so many fish were in the barrel.

Father prayed. Sgt. Bouchard looked at a picture of his sweetheart. The men either looked up to the heavens or down at the dirt beneath their feet and thought about the surer of the two.

"Fix bayonets!" The lieutenant shouted.

Hearts jumped, blood pulsed and hands trembled. Fear laughed in the face of courage. The men, ready or not, were going into no man's land. Bayonets were fixed on their rifles.

The German's were lined up too. They were supposed to attack right after the air cleared, but there were some communication errors and, now, the anxiety that built up at the beginning turned to exhaustion for them too.

The sun warmed the ground and the men about to face each other. A few men turned their heads up and let the sun warm their face, because for some it would be their last time to feel the sun on them.

No man's land was imposing. Barbed wire ends that hung out and waited to hook into unsuspecting men, bomb craters with metal shards and broken pieces of wood that waited to slice open or impale a man. Then, there were the bullets from the Germans' rifles that would shoot across the waste and strike a man so hard that they punched him and tore his guts or lungs or face apart.

Some men thought of no man's land as a monster's back with barbed wire for hair and huge abscesses that would be filled with the bodies and blood of men. When the monster shook the ground, the men were terrified.

The lieutenant blew his whistle!

The soldiers' hearts missed a beat and then the men climbed up and onto the mounds of sandbags that were there for their protection.

"CHARGE!" The lieutenant roared!

Sgt. Bouchard pushed Father back so that he would be behind the men.

The men half ran and half fast walked around the barbed wire. They stopped, aimed and shot at the German line.

The Germans, exhausted, snapped to when they heard the whistle. They launched a mortar barrage! "BOOM!" The mortars weren't nearly as horrible as the big bombs, but the blasts easily shredded a man's leg or tore at his skin. "BOOM!"

Dirt was thrown up and around the French soldiers who ran across the monsters back in no man's land. The monster twisted and turned to get those men off its back!

"CHARGE!" The lieutenant yelled again. He had his pistol out and shot.

The Fisherman aimed and shot; a French soldier fell. He aimed, exhaled slowly and pulled the trigger; another French soldier fell.

The French soldiers found it easier to shoot as the monsters back had deeper crevices where the soldiers disappeared and then reappeared in seconds with some cover around them. When they reappeared, their rifle was up and they shot!

A German soldier's head snapped back and then he fell to the ground behind him!

The German sergeant yelled, "CHARGE!"

Father was up and over the sandbags. He stumbled several times over dirt mounds, broken pieces of wood, a horse's leg bone that stuck up from the ground and he tore his robe on a strand of barbed wire.

"Dear Lord," he mumbled and saw the soldiers some distance ahead of him. They were dark stick figures that made archaic strides across no man's land. A bullet whizzed past Father's face. He swallowed a huge gulp and then stopped.

"BOOM!" A mortar exploded nearby. Chunks of dirt and dust covered him.

Rifle shots rang out all around him!

Father walked on and clutched his cross tightly. Then, the reality that the bishop told him about struck hard this time. A man lay just meters away and tried to turn to his side. Father shook his head and got his wits back. Then, he ran to the man, "MEDIC!"

When the man rolled back over, Father's eyes widened. "Dear God," he looked at the ragged gash across the man's stomach where his fatty tissue pushed out in a sudsy foam of blood and oxygen. "Dear God," he said again. "Just lay still." He pulled at the man's jacket to cover the wound and the man screamed!

"Sorry, so sorry!" Father looked around, "Help!" That's when truth overcame Father. The man was going to die. Father got his bible out and put his mouth to the man's ear. He whispered the last rites and then listened as the man took in his coming death.

"Forgive me, Father." The man said.

Father hurriedly went on and when he put his ear to the man's mouth, there wasn't any breath left. "Go in peace my son." He didn't finish, but what could he do? He bowed his head. "Dear Father, I did not have enough time … I'm so sorry, but please give his soul peace and comfort." He got a hanky from his pocket and wiped the dirt from the man's face. Once the dirt was off, there was a boy's face.

"BOOM!" A mortar landed nearby and the shockwave knocked father over! He shook his head to get his wits back, but his ears rang and that dizzied his mind.

"Father," he looked around and saw more men fall. He had to get up, he had to get to them and help them. "Get up you fool!" He looked at the open eyes of the young man and closed them. Then, he got up and walked towards the next man. The ringing in his ears made him walk off to the left. Then, he got his footing and hurried to the man who lay a meter or two from him. His eyes welled up at the sight of the man and he put his fingers on a bullet hole in the man's coat.

The fighting raged in *silence* around them.

Several bullets had ripped holes in the man's coat. He was dead.

"Please, forgive him his sins, bless him and keep him." Father pushed the torn cloth back on one hole and then stopped.

"People must know … to know, they must see." He stopped, looked up and mumbled, "Please forgive me father." He got his camera out and took a picture of no man's land. Then, he took a picture of the soldiers that fought on. Then, he took a picture of the bullet riddled body at his feet. He gasped, put the camera away and then marched on.

The *silence* broke and the fighting raged on!

The lieutenant lay in a crater with three soldiers. They looked at him for guidance. A fellow soldier was shot nearby, fell down and rolled into the crater with them.

"Lieutenant," Sgt. Bouchard said and helped the wounded man. "Is it enough?"

The lieutenant pounded his fist on the ground, "damn!" He edged up just enough to see, put the whistle to his mouth, his cheeks swelled and he blew!

The French soldiers didn't wait for the lieutenant to finish blowing that whistle. They turned and ran back towards their line. To avoid being shot, they ducked and dipped with every footstep.

The Germans did not resist the temptation to shoot retreating French soldiers. Some French were shot in the back and died where they fell. Other men were shot and wounded. Sgt. Bouchard grabbed a man by his bandolier and dragged him back.

"C'mon then!" Bouchard yelled, "You're not dying here!"

The Germans chased the retreating French into no man's land, but they were stopped when the French big guns began again. The lieutenant looked at his watch. He'd lost track of the time and didn't realize until now that they were in the kill zone of their own guns.

French bombs whistled through the air! The sound ripped into every single man in no man's land from the French soldiers to the German soldiers. "BOOM!" The seventy-five-millimeter gun fired much faster than other guns and the bombs landed all around them. "BOOM!"

The German's got the order to retreat and rushed back to their trenches. Then, several seventy-five-mm's guns shot! "BOOM!" "BOOM!" "BOOM!" The shrapnel tore at the German soldiers that ran back and killed them in no man's land.

Chapter 7: Nighttime Cries

Father gave last rites to a man and the man forced a grin.

The man choked on his words with bits of blood pooled around his mouth. "I've done my duty."

"Yes, you have." Father touched his face, "go in peace my son."

Father touched his camera. Soldiers ran towards him. He got his camera up and took pictures. First click, three men of which one was carried between the two. Second click, Sgt. Bouchard dragged a man with no left arm. Third click, the lieutenant turned, stood tall and shot his pistol at the Germans just as a mortar landed some meters nearby! Father put his camera away and ran to Sgt. Bouchard. "Let me help!"

"You were never to come this far!" Sgt. Bouchard yelled.

"Philippe, God wills me to go and death is there no matter." He got hold of the man and they lifted him up. "I've got you."

"Father," the man uttered.

Father caught a glimpse of where the limb had been blown off from the bicep down. His stomach turned and rolled to tell his eyes to look elsewhere.

They were back at the trench and attended to their wounded. The charge did what it was supposed to do, keep the Germans from gaining any ground.

Some hours later, near the end of the day … Philippe sat with the lieutenant.

The lieutenant's face was a map of dried blood and dirt. His bloodshot eyes teared and he wiped the tears away with a dirt ridden glove. "Damned orders."

"And the *damned* men." Philippe rubbed his temples. His face was as rough-hewn, his eyes were sunken and his cheeks were boney.

"It was meant to draw them out into no man's land." The lieutenant said.

"Then, our artillery …"

"Would hit them and break up their line." The lieutenant stepped out from the command tent and looked through the field binoculars. "How many?"

"A guess?" Philippe asked.

"Please," the lieutenant panned no man's land.

"Ten, maybe twelve dead." Philippe said. "There are wounded on the back of the beast."

"My God," The lieutenant said. "We'll have to send …" He looked at Philippe. "Sgt. Bouchard, organize a group of men, two teams with stretchers." He got a piece of paper, "I'll write and see to the German's that they allow us to get our wounded."

"Sir," Philippe said and then left.

It was dark now; the sky was full of stars and a few clouds that wore thin veils passed quietly by.

In the quiet of the night, men left in no man's land cried out for help. One to the left, one to the right, one just ahead of the two and another somewhere near the German line.

Father stood near a ladder and stepped up.

"Father," Philippe said and hurried to him. "Where are you going?"

"Someone's got to go out there and get them." He stepped up.

"There's no way to get to them yet, you'll be killed the moment the Germans see you." Philippe pulled at Father's robe.

"I must try." Father said and held a white cloth in his hand.

"The lieutenant is working to get the Germans to let us get our wounded." Philippe said.

"And that will be by morning … or later." Father climbed another step. "They'll be dead."

"This is madness!" Philippe grabbed Father's cassock with both hands and pulled at him.

"Let go!" Father kicked at him and then came down. They looked at each other and their fiery eyes glowed.

"I'm responsible for you." Philippe said. "If you go, I must go."

"And you're afraid to go … that's it, isn't it?" Father said and raised his chin.

Philippe spat. "You say that to me?" His teeth played with his lip. "Today was my eighth march into no man's land." He pinched his nose and blew. "Eight times, I've gone and faced the bombs and the bullets, dragged back half dead friends and passed men I could not carry … but you say, I'm afraid?"

Father lowered his chin, "I … I have misspoken myself. My heart and faith are driving me." He said.

"My love and love for my life drive me." Philippe said.

Two men cried out for help, "Ah!"

Father turned sharply. "When will the lieutenant know?"

"Now, it's likely the men will have to suffer through the night." Philippe said and pursed his lips.

"Let's rest ... just a short while." Father turned to his shelter. "If you hear something, tell me ... I want to go."

"Of course," Philippe said and nodded at him, but he waited to see that Father went to his shelter.

"Good night, then." Father said. He lay on his cot for a few minutes and then dimmed the oil lamp. He listened and heard mumblings of men. He got up, checked for his bible and his camera. Then, he quietly went back to the ladder. The white cloth was there on the rung. He got it and slowly climbed the ladder. A look to the left, to the right and then up at the heavens, "Dear Lord," he bowed his head, "please protect the men until I get to them." He climbed up, bent at the waist and then went over the sand bags.

In that moment, there was some rustling sound and a soldier quickly looked at the ladder in the distance. He studied it and then the top of the ladder, but there wasn't anything.

Father lay flat across the ground and inched away from the French line. The monster's back didn't quite feel the hard, fearful thumps of Father's heart as it beat through his chest and into the back of the beast in no man's land. He pushed himself ahead a foot at a time.

A man cried out some distance from him and he went to him. The ground was cool to the touch and the barbed wire nearby looked like ragged tree branches bent and broken; some moved with the wind and Father's heart jumped when one jabbed at him! He sighed, pushed ahead another foot and then another.

The half-moon was high enough to make out the ground ahead. He knew that the German lines were some distance yet. He stopped and caught his breath. Dirt crammed into his cassock; then, it soaked through to his body. Then, he moved again a foot at a time.

A man moaned nearby.

Father was startled and then got his composure. "Shh," he mumbled and leaned up. He spoke in whispers. "It's Father Leauvin."

"Father," the poor soul murmured.

"Don't talk." Father whispered and moved closer to the man. He didn't know just how far the German lines were, but an hour or so had passed since he left the trench. He turned his head to the right and lifted his ear up. The ringing wasn't nearly as bad now and he hoped to hear the mumblings or whispers of the German troops to know how close they were to them.

"I'm shot." The man said.

"Yes, but please … don't talk." Father said.

"I'm shot." The man spoke louder.

"And you'll be shot again if you're not quiet." Father's voice was quiet, but forceful.

He got right next to the man and got his mouth close to the man's ear. Then, he felt around until he found the man's hand; the man's hand was so cold, but he got hold of it and then whispered, "Tap my hand with your fingers, one for yes, two for no. Do you understand?"

The man tapped Father's hand once.

"Shot in chest?"

The man tapped once.

Father gulped. He must pull him back first. "Once shot?"

The man tapped twice.

"Shot in the stomach?"

The man tapped once.

"I'm going to pull you by your bandolier back to our line." Father quietly felt around and then got hold of the man's bandolier.

"Thank you," the man barely got out, the white mist of his words escaped his mouth and then faded into the darkness.

Father inched away as far as his arm would let him and then he pulled the man. The man's weight was a lot and Father reached out with his other hand and grabbed onto him. He pulled and, finally, the man moved.

The Fisherman moved his rifle slowly along no man's land. He had moved from his lower position when the French attacked to a higher position where he could see a lot of no man's land. In fact, he could sight all the way to the French lines.

Father pulled him close enough, moved away and then pulled the man to him. Then, he did it again until he moved at a pace that was equal to a snail's crawl.

"Father," the man spoke out.

Father nearly jumped, "shh." He put his mouth right against the man's ear. "Please, quiet."

The man tried to turn his head. He swallowed hard and then dipped his head, "going home."

Father's face paled, "Dear Lord." It was time. He spoke to the man quietly and offered him absolution and then anointing. "May the Lord Jesus Christ protect you and lead you to eternal life." He held the man's hand and the man gasped. Then, there was silence. Father wiped the tears from his eyes and fought his urge to sniffle.

The Fisherman stopped panning no man's land. He studied the black shadow hunched up and then down. His cross-hairs aligned with the form of a helmet. "Ah, you have come."

Father eased back down and looked the man over.

The man's eyes were closed and his body let out a soft pressed wind from his lungs. His last breath was on its way out.

Father's eyes widened and his skin bubbled up with goose bumps.

A faded pale white shadow of the man rose up from his body. He looked at Father, smiled and turned his head upwards.

"My Lord," Father said and, without thinking, sat upright and put his hands together to pray.

The image of the man went up and slowly came apart like threads pulled from a cloth until his soul was taken in by the night sky.

The Fisherman wiped his eyes and then focused on the man who knelt on the monster's back. "What's he doing?" He put the crosshairs on the creature and waited.

Father sniffled, "amen." He put his hand down and thought to lie down again, so that he could crawl back out. But he hesitated, got his camera out and unsnapped the cover. The click echoed across the hilly ground and down into the crevices. He looked at the moon and wiped his eyes. "To know his sacrifice."

The Fisherman's forefinger moved gently across the trigger, back and forth.

"Hans," a soldier whispered to The Fisherman. He raised his rifle and aimed.

"Nein, shh." The Fisherman said. He re-focused his cross hairs on the shadow of this person who tempted fate. "Was ist …"

The soldier next to him slowly pulled the bolt back on his rifle to check it was ready. Then, he slid the bolt forward.

The Fisherman sighed quietly, raised his hand and smacked the shoulder of the soldier. A hit to the helmet would have been heard around the world. "One more sound and I shoot *you*."

The soldier stopped.

Father moved the man's face and body so that the moon light was enough to brighten him. He slid around and to the side, and then he aimed the camera. He'd have to have the shutter open longer to take in more light. He didn't think on the danger and did not look at the German line.

A man cried out softly in the distance that was off to the left of Father.

The Fisherman sighted the noise; he had the man who cried out and paused. Then, he went back and sighted the strange creature that dare half stand in no man's land.

Father looked the man over, pressed the button and held it. The shutter was open and took in all that he was. Father counted quietly and then let the button release the shutter, "click."

The Fisherman thought and saw the motions of the creature with a box up to his face. "He … I think he's taken a picture." The end of the rifle dipped, but he was quick to re-sight the creature. "What madness is this?"

"Picture of what?" The soldier asked.

"Shut up, fool." The Fisherman's cross hairs were on their mark again.

"BANG!" A flare went up from the French side.

The Fisherman jumped slightly and then studied his target. The flare cast an orange glow over no man's land and the Fisherman closed one eye and squinted hard with the other.

Father, now, came to his senses. "My God," he turned to the French line and then back to the German line.

Someone shouted from the French side, "Get down!"

The Fisherman saw Father clearly, "It's their priest." He said and his cross hairs were on Father's chest. "What the hell is he doing there?"

Father dropped flat against the ground as the flare drifted overhead. The flare burned out in minutes. It was dark again.

Father moved around the man and headed for the other wounded man.

The Fisherman took his gaze from his rifle. "Their priest is there for the wounded." He wiped the dew from around his lips and stepped down from this higher position. "Let the priest be."

A couple of hours later, father was at the ladder and had the wounded man.

Philippe peered over the sandbags and shook his head. "Do not be the death of me." He helped him get the wounded man over.

Morning came and the Germans reluctantly agreed to allow the French to get their wounded as the Germans got their wounded too.

Father went out with the men and took pictures. His face had trails of mud across it where his tears drifted through the dirt. His body was numb when he was still and cried out in pain when he moved a muscle. He stood in no man's land. There were bombed-out craters, barbed wire ripped apart, a couple of donkeys that were chunks of dried muscle and bone, and there was the body of the man who died while being dragged back by Father. Father took a picture of the mules, of the landscape, and of the barbed wire. He hesitated and then looked up, "I must." He stood over the dead man whose jacket had several bullet holes in it and aimed his camera, "click."

The Germans watched Father through field binoculars. A couple of soldiers aimed their rifles and the Fisherman walked up.

The Fisherman looked at them as they aimed. "What are you doing?"

"The Priest." One soldier said.

"Ja?" The Fisherman asked.

"Why not let's shoot him." The soldier got his aim still. "They will send their men and we can get them."

The Fisherman shoved the soldier so hard that he fell down into the mud.

"Hans!" The soldier turned and got up. "What did you do that for!"

"Listen you; listen to me … all of you!" He looked at the other soldiers who gathered. "He takes pictures of this scheisse, of the dead …maybe of our dead." He shouldered his rifle. "You kill this priest and what will there be of the dead?" He shook his head. "Their souls will wander this miserable ground … lost forever."

The soldiers swallowed what the Fisherman said in a hard gulp.

"So, do not shoot that priest; he who will bless you when your time comes." The Fisherman walked off.

Several French soldiers with stretchers climbed over the sandbags. Philippe followed Father, but gave him some distance to wander.

The soldiers kept an eye on the German side as they would a wolf growling at them, with every fiber of their being. The Germans were out too and gathered their dead and wounded.

The French injured soldier who was to the far right turned his head as much as he could. He had a terrible leg wound that was a sticky-bloody mess with ripped pieces of his leg muscles hung out to dry.

"Please, I … I wish to take a picture of you." Father asked. "The men are coming and we'll get you care."

The injured man was dumbfounded and nodded.

Father took several pictures of the soldier and then a couple of pictures of the wound.

The soldiers who had the stretcher were dismayed and looked at each other.

Philippe shook his head and mumbled, "The priest offers a picture and no prayers."

"Father, wouldn't a prayer be more helpful?" One of the men asked. "We need to get him from here."

"Sorry, of course." Father and the soldier picked up the man. How he ever got so far from the attack to begin is a wonder; he was only three or four meters from the German line.

Father looked at several German soldiers who looked at him. He made the cross on his chest and dipped his head at them. "May the Lord help us all to find peace."

"They don't care about that Father." A French soldier said. "They are children of evil."

"Evil or not, I am a child of Christ and love my enemies." Father said, nodded and turned away.

"He has blessed us." The German soldier said.

Another soldier turned to him, "He must've seen that girlfriend of yours … you need a blessing."

The Germans' chuckled.

The French got to their lines, handed the wounded and the dead over.

Philippe stood between Father and the Germans at their trench.

Father got his foot in the rung of the ladder. "You're quite mad at me."

"I prayed and God said he would take my shift to watch you." Philippe grinned.

Father thought about the nighttime cries of the men. "It broke my heart to hear those men suffering and that there was nothing to be done."

Philippe took another look at the German line, turned and climbed down into the trench. He took a cigarette from his breast pocket; he popped it in his mouth and his lips played with it. "But something was done." He lit the cigarette and took a long drag. "You've saved them."

"Not all of them," Father said. "Their cries in the night will stay with me."

Chapter 8: Two Pictures, Two Men, One Woman

July 1916, mid-morning, the German attack was an off-again, on-again test of fire power and will. The Germans launched several more massive artillery attacks, but were repelled by French infantry and guns. Fortunately, there were no gas attacks this time. Word came that the Germans moved some of their artillery and infantry to the north along the Somme River where British and French troops amassed for an attack to end the war.

Father worried that Philippe would get orders to leave, but they did not come and Philippe was safe. Safe was relative to the surroundings in war, but Philippe was a friend.

Philippe got Father some military garb: a long coat, uniform shirt, trousers and boots which wore better than Father's black shoes. Father looked more like a soldier now than when he arrived. Philippe offered him a new helmet, but Father was adamant about the one he had on when a bullet hit it.

"No, no … I'll keep this one." Father said and ran his fingers over the dent. He'd found that a new habit was amiss to him until a soldier asked him about it.

"You don't know it, do you Father?" The soldier asked. A man barely five foot-eight whose cheeks were rosy red.

"What's that, Robert?" Father asked and felt the dent on his helmet again.

"Every time you go to take your pictures on the monster's back, you feel your dent." Robert laughed. "It's as if you do it for good luck."

Father smiled and then he thought about it. Yes, in fact he'd reached up there many times to feel that dent. "I never thought of the act." He shook his head. "But you've kept a good eye on me."

Philippe walked up, a little cleaner than usual. "Father," he rubbed his eyes.

"You've been to see your girl then?" Father asked and they shook hands.

"Yes, a nice break in Paris." Philippe rarely shared anything; no one knew the day of their death so to become good friends felt distant though Father cared about him a little more than the other men. He pulled his wallet out and looked at Father as if to question his motive to share something with him. "She's here." He took a picture from his wallet and showed it to Father. "A friend took the picture for her, a good picture."

"Oh," Father got the photo, looked at the woman and his skin cooled.

"You look quite surprised by her beauty." Philippe said.

Father's mouth clamped shut and he looked for the words to fill his mouth before it opened again. "It's ... she's beautiful, yes." Even in black and white, her full cheeks and lips made his heart jump. He wondered if he held the picture the same way months ago after he took it.

"Thank you, I love her very much." Philippe got the photo from him and looked at it again. "She is beautiful." He tucked it away.

Father felt sickly and looked down. He studied the dirt beneath him and it turned red, then it caught fire!

"Father?" Philippe touched his shoulder.

Father did not move his body, but his pupils grew along with the flames that ate up his boots, then the legs of his trousers and ...

"Father!" Philippe shouted.

"Yes," Father broke his gaze and rubbed his face hard with both of his hands.

"You were in another place." Philippe said. "I've told you not to think too much on the things you've seen. In fact, I don't think it's a good idea to take pictures."

"What?" Father said and ran his hands over one another. "Oh, well, but there must be some record, some respect to remember the men not just in our minds, but for other people who were not here."

"Our children?" Philippe had a scornful look.

"Perhaps, when the children are adults … they should know what happened here for the sake of not making war." Father took a deep breath.

"Perhaps," Philippe said. "Shall we go to the east end?"

"Yes, but I need something first." Father went to his dugout and got his camera. He looked at the entrance, took his helmet from his head and then got his bible out. He prayed, "Please forgive me father. It is not my faith that is shaken; it is a question of my vocation." He kissed the face of the bible and then touched it to his forehead. After which, he turned to Psalms and there was a picture. He looked at the entrance to his dugout again and then looked at the picture. It was the *same* girl. He paled. "Dear Lord," he uttered, put the picture back in his bible and closed it. He got his helmet firmly on his head and left.

Philippe and Father walked briskly to the east end. The east end was the farthest point from the command tent and the point closest by distance to the German lines. It was the one place where barbed wire was so thick a bird could make a nest one hundred times over.

"We should eat and then look to the men." Philippe said.

"Yes, that sounds fine." Father said.

It was a routine to take each day and, unless an attack dictated otherwise, visit different places along the trench or to leave their trench and go to one further away where Father could listen to the men. Father was a good listener and the men felt comfortable to talk about home with him now, to talk about life before they were here in the filth of war. In fact, when most of the men saw Father coming, it lightened their hearts now. Some happily posed for pictures even though Philippe didn't like the idea.

Philippe felt like the reality of war should be kept to the men who experienced it. The vileness of war, its ease at injuring, maiming and killing shouldn't be flouted to the public as a whole. He feared the average person's sensibilities would be corrupted and, therefore, put at ease in the face of violence. "So, the woman who sees a picture of a man's leg made into shredded meat is no longer bothered by such violence."

"That's a measure of a person's morals." Father replied, "They should always know it's bad to see or hear such things and not become comfortable with violence."

"So, you say Father, but I wonder if violence … this type of horrible thing in war would make them feel empowered by it." Philippe stopped and got a cigarette out.

"You wonder if a man or woman would feel powerful and be at ease to kill or hurt." Father's skin chilled.

"Yes, it's one thing to pull the trigger, but another to feel good about where the bullet hits." Philippe took a drag and blew it to the sky. "If a child sees the violence, they do not have the feelings to make it out to be as terrible from just a picture." He moved his hand around as he talked. "It's just a person and they are badly injured." He pointed at Father's leg, "but I blow their leg off and then they know how it hurts … this is war."

Father gulped. Their friendship had taken a turn in that Philippe was very open about his opinion. "Yes, but we can't do that." He wiped his brow. "In this military garb, the July heat is beating on me." He lifted his helmet and leaned against the wall of the trench. "Philippe, is it not possible that the person who tells the story gives it the power of pain and sorrow … that they make it real by the tale they tell?"

Philippe thought, "Perhaps." He didn't think so, but felt like he had to say so for Father's sake.

"If I say, bombs *blasting* the ground around us!" Father threw his hands up.

"Yes, but I know what it's like and that's not it." He took a long drag.

"But for them, as they don't know the reality, it's enough." Father waved his hands to clear the cigarette smoke.

"Sorry," Philippe twisted out the burned ashes. "We shall know in time."

"Yes, we shall." He tapped his camera. "If they do not like my pictures, then they can discard them."

"Not ones of beautiful women though!" Philippe laughed.

Father nodded and pulled his helmet down. He spent that evening taking pictures of other men, positions where the men stood guard for hours, some different angles of no man's land, the nest of barbed wire at the east end and some animals—horses and mules killed in no man's land.

The next day Philippe made arrangements for Father to see the medical tent near Fort de Souville. Father wanted to see the wounded men and the fort too.

"We may have time to get you near Fort de Souville." Philippe pointed east. "There's not much left of the place after the Germans first attack."

"Anything will do, maybe some pictures after I see the men." Father said.

They got permission and went to Fort Souville the first week of July, 1916. Father took pictures of the area; much of the place was blown up with only a few structures left to stand on their own. Father took pictures of wounded men; there were men who had large white bandages around their knee where the leg was amputated or blown off. Some men wore bandages over their eyes from gas blindness. Other men were missing an arm or both arms.

Father greeted every single man and talked to them before he asked about a picture.

Philippe found the matter annoying and didn't like the idea of taking the injured men's pictures at all. "Shall we make post cards too?"

Father half-grinned, "It's important to know these men."

Philippe shook his head and walked out of the medical tent.

They finished their day and headed back to their trenches further south.

The morning of **July 9th, 1916**, the Germans bombarded Fort de Souville with gas and a high explosive artillery barrage!

Father was in his dugout and got word from Philippe of the attack. "The men?" His bible rested under his helmet and his camera was next to both.

"They were moved before it began." Philippe said and took a drag from the little bit left of his cigarette. "My last one."

Father smiled, "I'm glad the men were moved to safety." He pinched his nose. "The smell is terrible."

"No worse than men who haven't had a proper bath in weeks." Philippe said and sniffed his underarm.

"As a priest, it's not for me to say." Father wiped the lens of his camera with a cloth.

Then, horror filled their hearts as a bomb whistled through the air!

"GET DOWN!" Philippe leapt and covered himself.

Father tried to grab his helmet from the table, but missed. "My helmet!"

"Get down, Father!" Philippe knocked Father's feet out from under him! Father lay with his feet near Philippe's head. "Leave the helmet!"

Father put his hands over his head and curled up.

BOOM! Dirt was thrown in the air and the ground roared in pain!

BOOM! Things in the dugout went up and then down! The table toppled over and spilled its guts on the floor: the bible, the camera and personal notes.

BOOM! Chunks of dirt landed around them and some men shouted about injured men.

BOOM! The ground shook again and again. BOOM!

"Damn them!" Philippe yelled. "Damn this mess!"

Bombs hit every place just ahead of their trench and behind their trench. Father's anxiety spiked with every whistle; this was the bomb and it said, "I'm coming down; I'm coming to get you!"

No man's land *was* the back of a monster that turned and twisted with every explosion! It kicked up dirt, it kicked up barbed wire, it shook and threw men from their places and it didn't care whether anyone was maimed or killed.

Nearly an hour later and the bombing stopped.

"They've used their budget of bombs for the year I hope." Philippe said and tried to rub the ringing from his ears. "Stay still, Father … just till the all clear."

"I don't think I can move yet." Father's legs were jelly; his heart beat hard and was terrified. "Fear has a God like grip on me."

"War gives fear power." Philippe said. He turned and saw Father's helmet on the ground with the camera next to it. The bible, which was flipped open, sat there too. "Here." Philippe reached over, got the helmet, shook off the dirt and handed it to father, "your helmet."

"Thank you," he got hold of it and put it on.

Philippe smiled at the sight of the camera with the case open. Had the film been exposed and ruined? Perhaps, it was broken and that was the end of it. A priest should give comfort, not take pictures, he thought. Then, he looked at the bible and saw the page, PSALMS. Something next to the bible caught his eye too, the serrated white edge of something the size of pack of cigarettes. He looked at Father who lay still with his head down and then looked at the white thing. "They'll call clear shortly, better to wait."

"I've no problem with that." Father said and sighed. "It's as comfortable here as my cot."

"Surely," Philippe said, but didn't hear a word. His attention was on the white thing next to the bible. He reached out slowly; his fingers pulled at the ground and wound their way through the bits of rubble. Then, his forefinger got hold of it and then his middle finger was on it; together they pulled the white thing from its spot under the edge of the bible and to Philippe. He dragged it quietly back and looked at Father.

"After this, I think we should lunch." Father said.

Philippe saw that the white thing was a picture, but he couldn't make out the image yet.

"Philippe, lunch?" Father tried to turn to see him, but couldn't.

Philippe cleared his throat, "Of course, escargot, a fine *vin du blanc* and some fresh poisson."

Father laughed, "If only to have fish and white wine, though I've never really enjoyed snails."

"No?" Philippe looked closely at the picture, his eyes widened.

"The earthy taste is too much for my liking." Father said and laid his head on his arm.

Philippe studied the face on the picture and his own face warmed, then got hot. It was his girl, his wife to be. He looked at Father and then felt around in his pocket. Perhaps, he'd dropped his own picture by mistake, though the size of this one was, he thought, much bigger. He got his picture from his pocket and put the two side by side. The one that was on the floor was bigger, finer. He looked at Father whose boots were just ahead of him. "I never asked you, but do you have any family … I mean besides your parents that got you the camera, a sister perhaps?"

A curious expression took over Father's face, "No."

"ALL CLEAR!" A soldier shouted. "Sgt. Bouchard!"

Philippe quickly turned, shoved the photo under the bible and got up. "Finally," he looked at father and got his rifle in hand.

"Yes, finally." Father got up and turned. "Goodness, my bible!" He quickly went to his bible, got it up and then saw the picture. He tucked the photo into the bible and then looked his camera over. "Oh no," the camera case was open, but the camera itself was okay. "Just the case broke, tant pis," he looked at the crack and pursed his lips.

"Yes, to bad it's just the case." Philippe said and smirked.

"BOUCHARD!" The soldier yelled some meters from them.

"Yes!" Philippe looked father over and the heat on his face made his cheeks red. "Coming!"

"I'll see you shortly." Father said.

Philippe looked him over again and then left.

"Wounded!" Another soldier yelled.

Father set the table back up and then set his camera on it. He set his bible down and the picture fell out; the picture turned end over end as it glided slowly to the floor. Something was different about it. He quickly got the picture back in hand and looked at the entrance to his dugout. Then, he turned his attention to the picture, "what's this?" It wasn't nearly as big as he remembered. He placed it in the center of his palm and looked it over, "either my hand is bigger now or the picture has shrunk."

Chapter 9: Sophie Rousseau, Apt 9, Rue De Garibaldi - Paris

Dec 1915, mid-day, Sophie looked her hair over and pushed back her bangs. Her fleshy red cheeks and puffy lips were well accented in rouge against her brunette hair. She pushed up on her bosom and looked her ankle length dress over. She was on her lunch and enjoyed walks in a nearby park. She got her coat on, pulled up the collar and then donned a hat.

She strolled past the charming shops and apartments that lined the street until she was at the dirt path to the park. There, she made her way down a path where some people walked and talked. An empty bench called to her to sit and warm it for a short time. She accommodated, used a small cloth to wipe the bench and then sat down.

Across from her, a man took pictures of the trees, then of some children who ran around and then of just the people who walked past.

They caught eyes and she fought a smile, but he noticed and smiled back.

"I won't take your picture." He said.

She gasped, "I didn't say you could not." She turned slowly to look elsewhere.

"No, you misunderstand …"

"Or you didn't say it right." She looked his jacket and slacks over, not shabbily dressed.

"I'd ask before I took a picture of such a lovely lady." The man smiled, tipped his hat and nodded. "My name is …" He stared.

"You've forgotten your name sir?" She looked at passersby and then him.

"Michael Leauvin," he took his hat off and bowed his head. The heat from his chest was too much. He pulled at his collar to cool his chest and then straightened his tie.

"And what do you do sir?" She moved her mouth softly; her lips gently moved near a pucker and then a nice smile.

He looked up as if to think and then looked at her, "I'm a photographer."

"There's a living in such work?" She kept her legs tucked close to the bench, but not close enough to let the bench dirty her dress.

"Yes, there's somewhat of a living." He felt ashamed.

Her attention drifted to other people.

"And your name?" He swallowed to get the dryness from his mouth.

"Sophie Rousseau," she stood.

"May I have a picture?" He held the camera up as if it were the one to ask.

"Of course, but I shall have a copy." She turned slightly for a good profile and then dipped her chin just a touch.

"You're …" He gulped.

"Yes," her lips parted ever so slightly.

"Beautiful." He said, held his camera steady. "There's just enough light." He gently eased his finger on the button, "Click!"

"You flatter me sir." She looked around, her cheeks brightened and then she turned to him.

"Would you …" He searched for the words, searched beyond his vocation as a priest and past the numbness that bound his feelings in rope. "Like to go for a walk?"

"Yes, but I must get back within the hour." She said.

"You work?" He asked.

"Yes, with so many men at the trenches, women must fill their shoes." She said and waited for him to choose a direction. "Why aren't you at the front?"

His face cooled and his cheeks turned a rosy red. The words, 'I'm a priest' sat in his throat. "That particular call hasn't come." He said and swallowed the words, 'I'm a priest.' He turned, held his elbow out and dipped his head towards her.

She put her hands together. "You are more forward than most men."

"I'm so sorry; I hope I did not offend you." He put his arms down the sides of his body.

"No, you didn't, but we've only just met." She pursed her lips, "We will see what the days ahead hold for us."

The months ahead were more than Father Michael Leauvin imagined. He fell in love with Sophie and she fell in love with him. He told her of the priest hood and she was upset at first that he kept it from her, but came to forgive him.

They sat in a café near La Tour d'Eiffel.

"But how will we …" A waitress set espressos down for them. Sophie smiled at the young girl and then looked at Michael.

"I … I'm not sure …"

"Of us?" She leaned away.

"No, goodness no." He looked around and pulled at his collar; though he was dressed in jacket and slacks, he still felt the sensation of his priest's collar around his neck, "it's my vocation." He whispered. "I'm not sure that … of that calling."

"To Christ, to serve Christ?" She asked and her rose petal cheeks turned a deeper rouge.

"Yes, I'm not sure of my life." He said.

"And of us?" She ran her fingers around the saucer.

He touched his fingers to hers. "Of us, I am absolute."

They sipped their espressos and their eyes locked into one another.

"The bishop told me that it's likely I will go to the front." He sipped his espresso.

"My goodness," her skin, soft and delicate as a roses petal, paled.

"With the allies at France's side, it's likely that Germany will crawl back across our border and never return." He touched her hand again.

She took his hand and held it tightly. "We hope."

He gently moved his thumb over the top of her hand, "and pray for it."

Michael knew that the truth was upon him. He must choose between a life of service or a life with Sophie.

That evening at her apartment, Michael looked over a collection of pictures on the mantel. "You have a lot of pictures; funny that I've come here so many times and didn't take them in."

"I began collecting them after I met you." She came from the bedroom dressed in a light brown dress with lavender lace at the collar and at the base of the dress.

"Who's this?" Michael reached back as this particular picture was behind some others. He held Philippe's picture; he was in uniform. "Your brother?"

"My brother?" It was too late. "Oh," she grabbed the picture and went to the other side of the living room.

"Sophie, who is he?" Michael's face warmed.

Her eyes teared up. "Someone," she put the picture to her back.

"Someone?" Michael bit at his lip and crossed his arms. "A lover?"

"No, he was someone to me … a while ago …" She wiped her eyes.

"But you still have his picture." He said and tightened his crossed arms.

"I haven't had the heart to say good bye." She went to her room.

Michael's face was hot, his cheeks red and his knuckles white as his fingers curled up. He gritted his teeth and wondered what to do. "So, you can't say goodbye to this other man?" He went to the door and opened it. "I will then."

She charged out of the bedroom. "No, Michael!" She came to him, wrapped her arms around him with her bosom against his back. "His life depends on me! Please, please …" She held him tightly.

"How is it that his life depends on you?" He moved her hands off of him. "How?"

"He's in the trenches." She wiped the tears from her eyes. "When we met, it … it was nice, but he got his orders and proposed." She couldn't hold back her tears. "I couldn't let his heart break and then see him go to face the Germans' guns."

Michael's face cooled, "So, you did it to keep him going."

"Yes, I … it was the right thing to do, but I don't love him." She brought her hands together. "I swear it."

"There is no need to swear anything." He opened his arms and pulled her to him. "I was … upset that there was another man."

"Yes, there is another man, but not for my love." She looked at him and their eyes met. "It is for his life." Her hand caressed his cheek, "I love you."

He pressed his lips to hers and kissed. He leaned back slowly, pushed her hair to the side, "your beauty shines brightly inside and out." He kissed her again, "as my love does for you."

She closed her eyes and puckered her lips. He leaned in, pressed his warm lips to hers and pulled her bosom tightly against his chest.

Chapter 10: Battle of Verdun

August 1916, morning, the air was lukewarm and decayed; the smell of dead horses and bodies drifted into the trenches. Philippe cleaned his rifle and stared into nothingness. His eyes were gleaned over with a haze of bitterness and betrayal. What did Sophie know? His stomach turned as his hands moved gently over his rifle and then one of his hands began to tremble. Jealousy moved up and down his forearm to his hand where it shook the bone and muscle. He made a fist so tight that his bare knuckles turned a milky white.

Father read a verse from Psalms to comfort him. He thought of the photo and imagined that Philippe had his picture. Should he talk to him? Should he tell him what she did for him, the sacrifice she made of herself to keep his spirits up? He bit at his lip.

No, how would he feel if that was his love only to be told it was there for show and not for real. His face warmed. His hands came together just as his knees touched the ground and he prayed. "Father," his eyes quickly looked at the entrance and it was clear. Then, his eye lids fell shut and he began. "Dear Father, I have let my emotions take me where I was not, should not have gone." He tried to swallow the dryness in his mouth, "I sinned and I am a sinner." His hands tightened. "I love her." His legs ached, "I love you." He shifted to ease his knees that rested on something painful, a rock or piece of metal. "I don't believe, despite what I've seen, that this is my place." He pressed his folded hands against his forehead. "I'm not … I don't want to be a priest; the bishop was right." His eyes opened and he looked at the bible that lay before him. "I will do my duty until I leave this place." His legs pushed him up and he turned a page in Psalms. There was the photo of Sophie. "I won't confront Philippe about her." He turned and looked at the door. "Let him have his love … for now."

Philippe watched the lieutenant walk up, "Sir."

"There's word of a possible German attack coming." The lieutenant pursed his lips.

"Sir," Philippe pulled the bolt back and charged a round.

"Cleaned and ready then?" The lieutenant looked ahead and saw the other men. "See that the men are ready and Father." He looked Philippe over and his eyes focused. "You alright?"

"Yes," Philippe stood tall.

The lieutenant looked him over again. "You don't look yourself." He looked away and then back at Philippe. "I can give you some time if you like; let Sgt. Manseau look after Father."

"No, no … I'm fine, just looking for the day when this war is over." Philippe got his rifle up and shouldered it.

"And go to that pretty girl of yours." He said, "What's her name?"

Philippe's face warmed and his cheeks turned an ash red. "Sophie."

"Lovely name, I'm sure she's anxious to see you." He patted Philippe on the shoulder. "I'll see if I can let you go early on the next rotation." He smiled. "For now, let's not lose our focus."

"No, let's not." He grinned slyly. "Thank you, sir." He saluted.

The lieutenant saluted and walked off.

"Morning, Philippe." Father had his gas mask at his side, his dented helmet on and his web belt on.

Philippe looked him over and got a cigarette out. "You are quite the soldier now." He lit the cigarette took in a quick drag and blew it out.

"Yes, thanks to you." Father touched the camera case. "Is there a chance of some pictures?" He looked at the broken clouds. "Not bad light." He rubbed his unshaven face. "Wish I had some cream to shave."

"Me too," Philippe thought and looked into no man's land. "It's possible for pictures today."

"Oh, I'm not sure about no man's land though." Father said and stepped away. "I've greeted some of the men and they say there are rumors of a push by the Germans."

"This is always a concern, Father." Philippe took a longer drag that matched the time he spent on his thoughts. "Someone pushes us, we must push back."

Father turned to Philippe and looked him over. "I suppose." He went to a pair of field binoculars and looked. "Seems quite clear." He took his gaze from the field binocs and looked at Philippe. "I hate that dreaded whistling sound the bombs make."

"But this is a good thing." Philippe exhaled and the smoke blew right in Father's face.

"What?" Father's eyes widened and he coughed.

"How else would we know to take cover?" He took another drag and appeared so very calm. "If the bombs came with no noise, like the despicableness of a crook who sneaks into your home and takes your precious things, how would we know to protect them, protect ourselves?"

Father didn't realize his breath stopped, he gasped. "Of course, I didn't think of that."

"No, you didn't." Philippe got to his feet. "Let's go."

"Is everything alright?" Father asked.

Philippe stopped and turned, his face was expressionless. Had his eyes been closed and his skin pale, Father might have thought he was dead. That moment, they were in each other's face. "It's war. Things are never alright." He locked his eyes with Father's eyes and then turned. "The men on the western end made some mention that you spend more time to take photos than to hear them."

"Sorry, I … I'll go to them." Father said and followed Philippe to the western end of the trench. It was a long walk with many twists and turns. He wondered if Philippe knew and if he knew about him and Sophie … what would he do, if anything?

They made their way to the western end and were greeted warmly by the men. Father spoke in confidence to a few men; there was no confessional so he walked with them to a spot with some privacy and listened. By the afternoon, Father spoke with twenty or so men and many were worried about another German push. They were especially worried about a gas attack. Even with the new M2 gas mask, someone would get gassed.

"Remember that it is not just you here; your fellow soldiers are here and we should all look out for each other." He looked at each face.

"Yes, we should." Philippe said.

"Let's pray please." Father bowed his head.

Philippe looked at Father as he prayed and felt his hand tighten around his rifle, his finger edged into the trigger guard while his other hand brought the barrel up slowly. His conscious took hold of him and he jumped. The rifle slowly returned to its safe place and Father said, "Amen."

They went to the HQ tent for mail call. Father had two letters and he nodded at Philippe as he passed to go read them.

The soldier in the command tent looked at Philippe, "smells nice." He handed Philippe the letter.

Philippe took the letter and walked away to the supply line trench that went to the very back of their lines. He opened the letter, "Dear Philippe," and read on. His cheeks sagged and his thumb and forefinger pressed together hard with the letter between them. His teeth gritted and made a sound of two pieces of broken glass that rubbed against one another. "Damn you." He muttered. The letter crumpled up easily in his grip. He got hold of the letter so that an edge hung out. He took a deep drag of his cigarette and then touched the end to the paper; the paper burst into a single flame and then ash. She did not say that she was in love with anyone else, only that she no longer loved him and wished him well.

Father tore up the letter from the bishop and put it in a fire bin. Then, he opened the letter from Sophie. "My love, I've told Philippe it's over and nothing more." He let the letter fall into the fire bin.

The lieutenant looked over the current lines that made up the French side and the German side. "They will come again and break the stalemate."

A soldier next to him shook his head. "They will throw what they have, all of it, at us."

"Yes, all of it." The lieutenant wrote a note. "Runner!"

A young man hurried in.

The lieutenant handed him a note, "let your feet move you quickly."

"Sir!" The young man was gone just as he got the letter.

"Get Sgt. Bouchard." The lieutenant ran his hand over the map of no man's land.

"Sir." The soldier left.

Philippe got to the command tent and saluted, "Sir."

"Keep Father close. It's likely he'll be needed sooner than later." The lieutenant said and looked downcast.

"So, that's it then?" Philippe looked at the map.

"Yes, they believe it may come just before nightfall." The lieutenant ran his hand along their lines. "Check weapons, ammunition and flares and be sure of water for everyone."

"Sir," Philippe saluted and then headed to the positions.

Father came in to the command tent.

"Afraid you just missed him, Father." The lieutenant said. "I suppose I should tell you as you're here." He looked Father over. "It's likely that the Germans will stage a major attack soon."

"I see." Father put his hand in his pocket and on his bible.

"It's likely there will be wounded and there will be …" He looked away.

"Of course, I'll … I am ready." Father gulped.

"You'll be in good hands." The lieutenant looked at the doorway just as Philippe came in. "Ah, Sgt. Bouchard. I've told Father to be ready."

"Very good, Sir." Philippe didn't look at Father. "Sgt. Manseau took the western end and the supply depot."

"Thank you, sergeant." The lieutenant nodded.

Philippe and Father left. They walked along the trench to the northern end this time. Father visited with some men there and then sought to rest before the long night. So, Philippe and Father parted until later in the day. They parted in silence, a nod to each other.

That evening the runner came down the trench at a heated pace. "Sir!"

"Easy corporal." The lieutenant looked the letter over. "My God." He looked at the soldier next to him. "Fort Souville is under attack, check our positions again."

"Sir!" The soldier darted from the command tent.

Philippe came to Father, "There is word that the attack will happen here most likely tonight."

There was a buzzing sound from no man's land, above no man's land! Several German planes flew high over them, but dropped no bombs.

"What's that?" Father asked.

"Reconnaissance, before nightfall," he answered. "Have your helmet, your gear ready. We won't know if it's gas or HE until it happens."

Oil lamps began to glow in the trenches. The sun was terrified and fled west.

"Of course," Father got his helmet and checked his gas mask. "Thank you, Philippe."

Philippe nodded and stepped out. He stood for a moment, looked back towards Father and spat. He got a cigarette and it was the last in his pack. His hands were still and he lit the cigarette, tossed the match to the ground and took in an easy drag. The smoke drifted from his mouth like a lazy passing cloud into the air where it faded into nothingness.

A gross whistling sound soared across no man's land! "COVER!"
Someone shouted.

Father ducked near the table and Philippe pushed up against the side of the
trench! BOOM! Then, there were several more bombs that whistled through
the air, BOOM! BOOM! BOOM!

French artillery returned fire and bombs soared past the French trenches.
The bomb blasts made the back of the beast spew dirt and rock!

BOOM! BOOM!

Philippe and Father attended to the wounded. The Germans hadn't begun
their infantry attack yet and it was after midnight when the shelling stopped.
Exhaustion dragged on the men and it had the help of filth and stench which
clung to the men in the heat. Sweat drifted down their brows and bodies just
under the men's uniforms; it crawled along at a snail's pace pulled on by
gravity alone and with every move there was an equally annoying itch that
made a soldier want to scratch desperately.

The lieutenant stood by a ladder and looked at the men to his right and left.
He wiped the sweat from his brow and sighed. "This is it men." He blew his
nose into the air, "relief tomorrow ... get through this night and then rest."

Father stood further down with Philippe who checked his rifle.

"The lieutenant has said for us to wait until they are half way." Philippe
didn't look at Father.

"Why?" Father was impatient.

"Do you wish to carry a rifle then?" Philippe shook his head.

"No, but I should go with the men when they go." He bowed his head.

"If it were possible, I should see you there with them and charging ahead." He felt his pocket and then realized he had no more cigarettes.

The lieutenant looked at his pocket watch in the moonlight. "Ready flares, pass the word for a few moments after the whistle."

Soldiers passed the word down the line and dreaded an assault at night; it was hard enough to shoot the enemy during the day with bombs blowing up around you, barbed wire that grabbed and tore their bodies and Germans shooting at them. It would be hell.

"When we go over men, it's possible the Germans will be right at our door." He looked up and down the line. "Keep your wits about you and be sure that the flares go far ahead of us!"

"BANG!" A shot rang out and cast bits of dirt from a destroyed sand bag.

"My God!" Father let out and ducked.

Philippe smiled, "really Father … you're quite safe."

Then, several shots rang out! The attack had begun!

"Fix bayonets!" The lieutenant looked at his pocket watch again.

German bullets ripped up the sandbags and the ground around them.

Hands trembled and tears came down scared eyes.

"READY!" The lieutenant put the whistle to his mouth.

Dozens of bullets shrieked past their heads!

He blew the whistle and the men went up the ladders! One man was shot the second he crawled up! His body fell limp, crooked backwards and fell back into the trench!

"GO!"

Onto the sandbags and into no man's land! Dozens of French troops leapt up and charged ahead! The lieutenant blew the whistle one more time to ensure the charge. "ATTACK!"

Philippe was not able to sit this one out with Father and so he went up and over.

Father looked up and down the trench. "My God, please watch over and protect who you can!" He got to his feet and climbed the ladder, "amen!" He went up and over!

Bullets zinged past and mortars hit here and there! The shockwave blew men from the ground they were on! Father got to an injured man and looked him over. He had holes in his shirt, bullet wounds. Father got him by his bandolier and dragged him back to the trench. "Come on then!"

BOOM! A mortar hit a few meters from them and knocked Father to his knees, "damn!" He shook his head and tried to get to his feet, but fell back down. A few seconds passed and he got to his feet, grabbed the man's bandolier and drug him back to their lines. He turned to pull the man over and saw that half of the poor man was gone. "No," Father wiped his face and BOOM! Another mortar landed some distance away! The blast threw dirt and shrapnel at them!

Then, he heard the cries of other wounded. He stumbled across the hilly ground and his feet got tangled up in barbed wire. Bullets ricocheted off of a cart and struck the ground around him. Where were their men? He got his foot free and kicked at the barbed snake that tried to coil around him. "Stop it!" He hurried to a soldier and grabbed him. "Are you shot?"

"Of course!" The man shouted.

"I've got you!" He grabbed the man's bandolier and pulled hard.

Sweat dripped down his face and he swallowed the salty bits every time he took a breath. "C'mon!"

"Yes, keep going!" The man shouted.

Father got him to the sandbags and shoved him over! "WOUNDED!" He turned and went back.

The French soldiers shot and ran at the German line, but it wasn't going to happen for them. They would not rout the Germans from their trenches.

More mortars hit! BOOM! BOOM! BOOM!

Father fell to the ground and into a bomb crater with his hands over his helmet.

Philippe dropped right next to him. "You'll get no pictures laying here, Father!"

"I will surely die out there!" Father said.

BOOM! BOOM! The second whistle for retreat blew. French soldiers retreated and the Germans shot as many French in the back as they could! Bullets zinged past.

"No, Father ... not out there." Philippe raised his rifle and pointed it at Father. "Go on, go take your pictures!" Philippe's eyes glowed red in the reflection of flares that bursts overhead.

"Are you mad!" Father pushed up on his side.

"No, Father. I'm quite sane." He aimed at Father's chest. "You and my Sophie are lovers, you have slept with my wife to be!"

"I …"

BOOM! BOOM! The German bombardment was heavier and the French artillery responded in kind!

"Go take a picture, because you are no priest." Philippe motioned with his rifle for Father to go. "What man calls himself a servant of God and loves another man's woman!" He rolled to his side to have a better shot. "You are the devil!"

"She doesn't love you!" He stammered, wiped the sweat and dirt from his forehead and then looked around for other soldiers to come to his aid. There were no soldiers.

BOOM!

"Yes, you convinced her of that! You, a priest …" Philippe shook his head. "Well, you'll not have her." He edged up.

BOOM! More bombs, more bullets bounded across the air and landed all over no man's land!

Father looked at the rifle and the distance. "Don't do this, don't commit this crime."

"You dare to say that to me!" Philippe aimed at Father's head.

The Fisherman panned no man's land and shot! A French soldiers uniform puffed out and he fell. "Stupid to attack our lines, so stupid." He panned the ground and looked for survivors. Then, a flare went up right by him! "Damn it!" He quickly closed his eyes and then re-focused. There was someone who stood with no rifle, "look at this fool." He aimed and put the cross hairs on the man's side. "Turn for me."

Father got up and stood. "I'll not be murdered by you, Philippe Bouchard."

"You're right, you'll die by enemy fire and then I will go home to her." Philippe said and edged up to sight Father better. "She will have no choice then."

"What's this madness?" The Fisherman looked the man over and saw a box in his hand. "The camera?"

BOOM! BOOM! More mortars and then more flares!

Father was knocked to his knees. "We'll both die here!"

"Yes, that's possible." Philippe and Father's eyes locked. "Go take that picture, now!"

Father got his camera from his side and held it at his waist.

The Fisherman put his crosshairs on the box, "that damned priest is there now?" Just off to the bottom of his crosshairs, he saw the end of a rifle. "What's this?"

"Go!" Philippe yelled and got to his knees. "Take a picture."

Father looked around for something to photograph.

Bullets zinged past him and one ripped the edge of his shoulder.

"AH!" He was grazed and felt the wound. Then, he turned to Philippe. "I am wrong for what I've done, but she did not tell me at the beginning."

"Liar!" Philippe edged up. His head and shoulders were just above the crater. "You lie!"

"No, Philippe." Father said and stepped back. "I'm sorry, truly, but I do not lie."

"You are sorry." Philippe aimed at Father's chest.

"BANG!" White smoke drifted into the sky.

Chapter 11: The Camera

Father recoiled, but not from the bullet. Rattled nerves possessed him and he shook terribly. His eyes were closed and he slowly opened them.

The mortars stopped and a couple of soldiers shot at each other, but there was a growing quiet.

Father caught his breath. He muttered, "Dear Lord." Then, he felt his chest and nothing hurt or felt destroyed. "Has he shot me?" His eyes looked up from the dirt and kept going until they met Philippe's eyes, a cold glare from a man who lay back against the ground. "Philippe?" He turned and looked at the German line.

Something moved him to look at Philippe again and he turned his head. A milky white cloud drifted out of Philippe's body and hovered over it.

Father dropped to his knees and studied the apparition. "I'm sorry, Philippe." He brought his hands together and made a cross over his chest. "May the Lord Jesus Christ protect you and lead you to eternal life ..." He looked up, "Dear Lord, I ask you to please forgive this man his sins, amen." The apparition drifted up where he met eyes with Father. For a moment, the cloud of the man who was Philippe on earth hung there and its eyes were locked with Father's eyes. Then, he turned upwards, drifted into the darkness where the cloud faded and he was gone. "Goodbye, Philippe."

Father got to his feet and looked at the German line.

The Fisherman had his rifle aimed at Father, "No one is to shoot him! NO ONE!" He paused and the end of his rifle dangled in the air with its barrel pointed at Father. "What now Father?"

Father stood tall and made a cross over his chest. Then, he dipped his head in a blessing to them. "Let there be peace, amen."

The Fisherman saw Father make the cross at him. He set his rifle down, took his helmet off and knelt. "Dear Lord, we too pray for peace." He stood and got his helmet back on, then he picked up his rifle. "Until we meet again, Father."

Father, so shaken by everything, turned and stumbled a few meters. Then, he stopped suddenly, "the camera." He turned and went back.

"BANG!"

Father fell to the ground.

The sky lit up and a flare floated overhead.

Father got to his feet, looked around and saw his camera. He got it and went to Philippe. The sky was clear now with a strong moon, so Philippe was well lit. Father looked him over and pushed down the cloth where the bullet hit. Philippe's mouth was open, his cheeks were sunk and his skin was a fleshy white. "For others to know the truth of war ... that there is no good in it." He focused and put his finger on the button. A soft sigh pushed through his lips, "click." The camera paused and took in as much light as it could, then he let off the button, cycled the film, focused again and stepped to the side. Philippe's hand was not on his rifle. "No," he said, went to Philippe and moved his hand so that it was on the rifle and his finger on the trigger, "He died fighting for what he believed in."

"Click," Father knelt and looked Philippe's body over. Then, he got Philippe up and onto his shoulders. The rifle dropped to the side. "You'll not need it anymore." He walked off to their trench just as the flare fizzled to its end and darkness ate up no man's land.

The next morning, Father looked over his things: his helmet, his uniform, his bible and his camera. There, next to the camera, was his collar with brown stains from mud. He ran his dirty hands over his dirt ridden face and tried to push the horrors of last night out of his mind, body and soul. Had Philippe really been killed?

"Father?" The lieutenant stood at the entrance to the dugout. "Father, are you alright?"

Father's eyes had dirt caked up in their ducts. He rubbed it out and everything was suddenly blurry. "I'm alright."

The lieutenant stepped in. "Philippe only had this in his uniform." He handed Father the picture of Sophie. "Perhaps, you would consider writing a letter to her?"

He rubbed his eyes and the blurriness went away. He studied her face and smiled. "Yes, I will write the letter."

"Why don't you come have some coffee?" He looked at the trench. "We've been relieved, so the men will be leaving at the noon hour."

"God bless them." Father got to his feet. "I'll wash first."

"You look quite dirty." He chuckled and stepped out, "the coffee is fresh and hot." He walked away.

Father looked himself over, knelt, closed his eyes and prayed quietly. He opened his eyes, "Amen."

After coffee, Father read an order. He was relieved, like the men, but his relief was permanent; he was to return to Paris.

Father was in his cell at the church. He'd had a fresh bath and a good shave. He got up and looked at his cassock that hung in the closet. His collar was white and perfectly clean. He pulled the collar from the shelf, put it around his damp neck and looked in a small mirror. Then, he reached up and pulled it off.

The bishop waited for Father and looked up several times from his desk to see if Father was at his door. "Where is he?"

"I'm here, bishop." Father was dressed in street clothes.

"Why aren't you in your cassock?" The bishop got up and leaned over his desk. "Father?"

He pulled the collar out, walked up and set it gently on the bishop's desk. "I'm sorry, but this is not my calling."

The bishop took in a breath, stood erect and pulled his shoulders back. "I wondered." He sat down. "I saw in you the light that led down a different path, but no other man can tell you to go here or there."

"No, they can't." He had an easy, relieved grin.

"Then, go in peace my son … go in peace, Michael." The bishop made the cross over his chest.

"Thank you, your Excellency." Michael turned and left the church. Outside, the sun shined and the warm air lifted his spirit. "I'm coming." He said and hurried down the street with his bag in hand.

"Michael!" Sophie yelped. "You're back!"

They hugged and kissed, then held each other tightly. "It's done." Michael said.

She smiled and kissed him again. "I love you."

"I love you." He said and pressed his lips to hers.

She leaned back and turned to the mantle. There was the picture of Philippe. "I got your letter."

Michael looked at the picture. "He was a very brave man."

"A hero," she said.

"Yes, a hero." They kissed again. Michael knelt and their eyes met. "Will you marry me, Sophie Rousseau?" He took a small box from his pocket and opened it.

"Yes!" She bent over and hugged him, "Yes, my love!"

He was overwhelmed by her kisses. "Let's have a picture then." He put the ring on her finger. He got a stand and set the camera on it. Then, he got an extension and attached it to the camera button. They stood in front of the mantle with Philippe's picture to the side of them. They put their arms around each other and turned to face the camera. Father sighed softly, "smile." He had his thumb on the extension button, "click."

The End.

About the Author:

Michael Lachance writes fiction and his unique and wonderous characters bring life to each story.

Three Fools for Spies is a story about three friends who go to Europe and get caught up in a race against the Swiss police, United States secret agents, and Russian secret agents in a dangerous game of international espionage.

The Treaty of Versailles, The Power of Love is a story that evolved out of a trip to Poland and a prison camp. This story is about Erich and his love, Nikki. Prior to World War II, Nikki is arrested and imprisoned at a concentration camp. Erich will not let the man he loves die in the camp. In order to save Nikki, Erich must become what he hates most, a Nazi.

The Long Short is about two people who don't know each other until their flight to the US crashes. They end up on an atoll and have very different goals they want to achieve. Bill wants to find treasure and Claire wants to be rescued. One of them will get what they want at the expense of the other

21 Windows is about a family who buys an old farm house in the country. They discover a painted over window and a room hidden in the house. After they knock a wall out to get into that room, bad things happen.

Currently, Michael's working on *The Adventures of Skipper Pete* (YA-four books in the series), *Butch Roberts and The African Adventure* which is about a gay man who travels to south Africa in search of fun and adventure, but winds up on the run from a rebel army.

Published works are available in eBook or paperback!

To connect with Michael, please visit

Facebook – www.facebook.com/skipper.pete

Twitter - https://twitter.com/skipperpete1

Website: www.skipperpete.com

Please join him on his website blog for updates about novels in the works, pre-orders, and Q & A. Upcoming works include: Skipper Pete Adventure Series, So Happy, and Butch Roberts and The African Adventure.

Michael's books are available as eBooks and in paperback at all major book sellers: Amazon, Barnes & Noble, iTunes Book Store, Smashwords and other sellers.

Thank you for your interest and enjoy.